MW00932110

COWBOY'S INNOCENT ASSISTANT

J.P. COMEAU

Copyright © 2020 by J.P. Comeau

All rights reserved.

No part of this book may be reproduced in any form or by any electronic or mechanical means, including information storage and retrieval systems, without written permission from the author, except for the use of brief quotations in a book review.

❋ Created with Vellum

Bella

"Get the hell off me."

My dad's drunken voice echoed off the corners of my mind as I helped Mom get him off the couch. I blocked out Mom's soft tears as she sniffled. My heart broke for her, but I honestly didn't understand why she stayed with my foolish father. For as long as I could remember, he was nothing but a pathetic drunkard who kept getting worse and worse as the years went by.

And as I helped lug him up the steps, I felt exhaustion settle into the marrow of my bones.

"Come on, sweetheart. Just a little more," Mom said softly.

Dad threw his head back. "You should've just left me on the couch!"

I rolled my eyes. "Get upstairs, or I'm letting you tumble down these steps."

Mom gasped. "Bella!"

Dad hiccupped. "Told you. Don't none of you love me."

Not this version of you, no. "Just get your feet underneath you, yeah? Your words aren't slurred, so I know you can at least walk."

Mom cried the entire time we helped Dad up the steps. She sobbed in the corner while I undressed him before rushing to get a trash can when he started gagging. And after he puked all over himself, I was the one to clean him up while she had her existential crisis in the corner. For once in my life, I wanted not to have to be the strong one in my family. The more it happened, the more draining it became, and I felt my own life slipping through my fingers. College had been brutal enough, traveling back and forth from Dallas to clean up Dad's messes every single weekend.

Then again, it wasn't as if he had planned his rodeo accident.

"Come on, Mom. I have to get ready for work. Can you come stroke his hair until he falls asleep?" I asked.

She wiped at her tears. "Can't you keep doing it? He loves it when you do it."

I ground my teeth together. "Well, if you want to eat in a couple of weeks, someone in this house has to work. So, I'm going to need some help."

She slowly stood from her chair and tiptoed over, acting as if my father were some sort of entity that frightened her. And I got it. I understood where that fear came from. But, it sure as hell didn't help me out. I needed to be out the door five minutes ago, and I still hadn't finished getting dressed. I'd have to forgo jewelry and makeup if I had a hope or a prayer of getting to my new job on time.

And after tucking my father in, Mom and I exchanged places.

"Wait, sweetheart," she said as she grabbed my wrist.

I peered over my shoulder. "What is it?"

Her watery gaze met mine. "Thank you for all you've done for our family. I know I haven't stepped up like I needed to, but it's just hard sometimes."

I nodded. "I know it is."

"It's just—when you see the love of your life trampled like that, it does something to you."

I pulled away from her grip. "And as the love of his life, it's *your* wedding vows that tell you to step up for better and for worse, not mine."

I was harsh on her, but I'd dealt with this bullshit for the better part of fifteen years. At twenty-five years old, I could still remember watching my father take that spill in the rodeo arena when I was only ten years old. I could still remember the first time Dad had mixed his pain pills with his beer before projectile vomiting all over the dinner Mom had made for us that night. And I can still remember the fight it led to before Dad cracked his hand against Mom's jaw.

Of course, if anyone asked her about it, she'd just say he was drunk. Maybe a bit too high. But that he was getting better. And if by "better," she meant Dad was too drunk to swing his fists around, then she'd be right.

I didn't know how much longer my father's liver had, though.

Still, I pushed those thoughts from my mind as I finished getting ready for work. I heard Mom calling for me, but I acted as if I didn't. I couldn't lose this job. It had been hard enough to move back home to help out my family after getting my degree. It hurt enough to be taking some ignorant secretarial position instead of pursuing my passion like any other person my age.

And I sure as hell wasn't about to lose my new job because my mother didn't know how to run her own life.

I rushed out to my car and sped across town, parking with only one minute to spare. I gathered my things and took one peek at myself in the fold-up visor mirror, then decided I looked presentable enough. I locked the doors and rushed inside, looking around for the man who had hired me for the position in the first place.

Ryan Remington, I thought that was his name.

"Bella Lancaster?"

I turned at the sound of the unfamiliar voice and found a cold, towering man standing behind me. He had a briefcase clenched in his hand, and his free hand slid into the pocket of his stark navy suit. Everything matched, all one solid navy color from his tie to his cufflinks to his shoes. It all worked to accent the stoic stare on his face and the man's brooding brown eyes. And while he bore a striking resemblance to the guy who had interviewed and hired me, the darkness that fell over his features because of his brow line gave me pause.

My God, he's handsome.

"And you are?" I asked.

The man didn't bother sticking out his hand. "Wyatt Remington. I'll be the one onboarding you since my brother is currently taking paternity leave."

I nodded. "Well, congratulations to him."

He turned to face down the hallway. "Follow me and keep up. Take notes if you wish. This won't take long, though. Just a small tour around the facility before we get you set up at your desk."

As he walked me around the newly renovated former bank, I couldn't stop staring at his back. He seemed to tower over everyone and everything else in this place, and the shadow he cast was long and arduous. His shoulders rolled themselves back with a cool sort of confidence, and the way his tailored suit clung to his body made me want to lick my lips. Were all of the Remington brothers this fine? Because I swore, every time I laid my eyes on one of them, my mouth started to water.

Like it was in the presence of Wyatt.

I let my gaze linger down his back and marveled at the tight, perky globes of his ass. His long legs seemed strong beneath the silken, expensive fabric of his suit. And the cologne that trailed behind him made my heart flutter in my chest. I closed my eyes when we came to a stop at the restrooms and shook my head a bit, hoping to pull myself out of my trance.

But, when I opened my eyes, I found him staring at me. "Ready to continue, Bella?"

The sound of my name on the tip of his tongue sent a shiver down my spine. "Yeah, yeah. Sorry."

His stare fell down my body. "I hope you pay attention better than this when you're behind your desk."

I blushed with embarrassment. "You have my word that I will."

His eyes lingered on me a bit longer than usual. "I don't think I have to reiterate how important it is that you always be on top of your game. You're going to be the first face people see when they walk into Remington Petrol Headquarters, so you're going to be making the first impression on behalf of our entire company."

I swallowed hard. "Yes, sir. I fully understand."

He turned his back to me. "Good. Because we can't have anyone screwing this up for us."

I didn't know what had crawled up his asshole and died, but I shrugged it off. I was the only person in my family capable of holding down a job, so I had to suck it up. After taking me to each floor and briefly talking me through what their functions were, he led me back downstairs toward the main double doors that signified the building's front.

He then ushered his arm out toward a magnificent mahogany desk. "This is where you will perch," Wyatt said.

My jaw fell open. "Wow. This thing is huge."

"And we expect with all of the storage you have that you will see to it that your desk doesn't get cluttered. We want a clean-cut, professional appearance coming from your station. Understood?"

I walked over to it. "Understood."

"Wonderful. Your temporary login information for the software system we use in the building is taped to your computer screen. In the drawer beneath the phone is a headset as well as button assignments to transfer calls between offices and departments. You have the week to get settled in and used to things before we'll start holding you to a higher standard."

I let my hand slide over the buttery leather seat meant only for myself. "I can do that."

"Good. If you have any questions, my office is on the top floor. Just come up the elevator, walk to the end of the hall-way, and knock on the onyx door with the crystal knob."

Sounds tacky as hell. "I can do that."

And without another word, I smelled Wyatt's cologne drifting away, leaving me to ease myself into my new work chair alone with a smile on my face before my phone started ringing off the hook.

2

Wyatt

I stopped at the water fountain at the end of the hallway before I peeked back down the carpeted expanse. Bella Lancaster, the woman my brother had hired to fill our front-desk secretary seat, wasn't quite what I expected her to be. From her resume I had read through briefly this morning, I had gotten the impression that she was more of a timid woman. Yet, my first impression of her was a bit more spitfire than that.

It made me grin as I straightened my spine.

Her bright-red hair had been pulled back into a top knot at the crown of her head, leaving small wisps to frame her bright brown eyes. They seemed almost amber, and had I not been working overtime in my brain, I probably would have stared at them more than I had. Acting as cold as I did around her did the trick, though. She didn't even bother looking back at me, which was good. I mean, it wasn't as if I could go around thinking the girls here were hot. Not with us being in a professional environment.

From the second she turned around, though, she had caught my eye. The freckles smattered across her nose and cheeks were the cutest things I'd ever seen. Her lips were delicate but held a fierce and fiery tongue that already earned my admiration. Not to mention, the soft curves she kept hidden beneath her clothes. The dress she wore didn't cling as tightly to her as most of the girls who donned them in Conroe. If anything, her outfit with her cardigan and those flats she was wearing spun my head off its rocker as I envisioned what might be beneath them.

Get to your fucking office and stay there, idiot.

I pulled myself away from the water fountain and made a beeline for the elevator. I jammed my palm against it, all the while allowing my eyes to be dragged back to Bella's desk. I watched her slip on her headset before answering her first call. And when she pulled out the informational booklet I had put together myself, a grin spread across my face just before the elevator doors opened.

Finally.

I rode up the levels until the doors gave way again, almost as if to usher me straight to my door. Only Ryan, Boone, and I had offices here. The rest of the brothers had their offices established in the stables with the horses they trained. Why they'd want to be distracted like that was beyond me. But, it gave my brothers and me more space to stretch out when we had designed our offices.

And as I threw open the door to mine, the view of Conroe that unfolded before me comforted my raging mind. For a brief moment, Bella fell away from my thoughts. I closed the door behind me and tossed my briefcase onto the couch before making my way toward the tinted floor-to-ceiling windows that backdropped my desk. I slid my hands into my pockets and gazed out over the view I had. I could see for five or so miles, with houses and ranches spread out as far as my eye could see. With the sun casting golden rays over this beautiful small town, I drew in a deep breath, readying my mind for yet another busy day of tackling mine *and* Ryan's work.

After enjoying the caffeinated view that seemed to fill my body with energy, I eased myself down into my chair. And the first thing I did was pick up my office phone to dial Ryan's number. I wanted to check in on him. See how things were going with his and Ellie's new addition to their family.

And I was shocked when he picked up after the first ring.

"Things already falling apart without me there?" he asked.

I leaned back. "You fucking wish."

He chuckled. "So, what's the call for? Everything okay?"

I leaned back so much I found myself staring at the ceiling. "Can't a brother call to see how his family's doing?"

"Well, if I hadn't just seen you last night, it might not be so weird."

I rolled my eyes. "How's the little one? And Ellie?"

"They're both good. And Micah's adjusting very well, too. He already wants to take the baby swimming, and Ellie and I keep tag-teaming who tells him 'no.'"

I chuckled. "Sounds like hell."

"The best hell I could have ever wished for."

A pang of jealousy struck me in my gut. "Well, give Ellie and the rest of your family hugs for me. Want me to call around lunch?"

"You only have to field my work for me, Wyatt, not my entire life."

"Then, call me once you fuck up so I can help you clean it up."

He chuckled. "And there's that balance. I can do that."

I leaned back up in my chair. "Oh, and one more thing."

"What's that?"

Thoughts of Bella flooded my mind once more. "Can you stop hiring hot women to work for us? It's practically torture over here."

"Ah, so I take it you met the new girl?"

I licked my lips. "Just hire some ugly ones the next time we need to fill positions, all right?"

He barked with laughter. "Pretty sure I can't discriminate or refuse employment because of what someone looks like."

"Hey, if you don't tell, I won't, either."

"Get the fuck out of here," he said through his laughter, "we'll talk soon. I promise."

I grinned. "Sounds like a plan. Enjoy your time off."

"Yeah, but don't you start enjoying all of these hot women. The last thing I want to come back to is a slew of sexual harassment allegations I have to investigate."

I rolled my eyes again. "Bye, Ryan."

He mocked my tone of voice. "Bye, Wyatt."

I dropped my office phone back into its cradle before turning to face my computer. I logged in and started clicking around in Ryan's email that he had given me permissive access to while on paid leave. And as my fingers started flying across the keyboard to answer everyone, I drew in a sobering breath.

I enjoyed the longer workdays, such as this one. It helped me to forget about how empty my life was once I left this place. It helped me forget that my life was devoid of meaning outside of this building. For years, I had thrown myself into work, building my wealth, watching my investments, and putting all of my free time into growing this company beyond our parents' wildest imaginations.

I enjoyed the days I worked myself to the bone. Because then, all I did when I got home was fall into bed and sleep, instead of staring at the ceiling and contemplating where the hell I went wrong in my life.

For starters, I wasn't a big rodeo guy like the rest of my family. I was always kind of the black sheep, in that regard. While my family was training horses and spending all day sweating it out in the hot summer sun just to watch a bunch of men race animals or whatever, I curled up beneath the bleachers of those same rodeo stands and read books. Sure, I cheered for my family whenever they were racing, but I had no passion whatsoever to be the one on the horse in the first place.

Hell, I only rode horses for pleasure. And I didn't own any of my own, to boot.

Focus, Wyatt, like what you told Bella to do. You're getting off track.

I doubled down on the email responses before quickly flipping over to my own. I continued typing back and answering questions until my fingers were blue at their tips. Then, I started sifting through paperwork. There were mounds of it, and it made me smile as I slid the first folder off the top. But, just as I flipped it open, a knock came at the door.

"What?" I called out, and I heard it ease open.

"What do you mean, *what?*" Bryce's voice caused me to look up.

"Hey there. Everything okay?"

He held up two bags of food. "We have lunch plans, remember?"

I blinked. "It's lunchtime?"

He stepped into my office and closed the door. "Actually, lunchtime was fifteen minutes ago. What the hell are you doing?"

I flipped the folder closed and put down my pen. "Just working. You know, catching up on mine, as well as Ryan's, stuff."

Bryce sat in a chair in front of my desk. "Well, take a second to scarf down some food before everyone starts to think you're a robot."

I grinned. "Hey, that might be fun. You never know."

He started divvying up the takeout. "You're a workaholic; you know that? You and the rest of your brothers, for that matter."

I blinked. "You think Boone is a workaholic?"

"If by that, you mean Boone is the fun one on your side of the family? Then, yes."

I chuckled. "I can't even argue that point."

He handed me my sweet tea. "Good, because it's a valid point."

Then, another knock came at my door, and it perked up my ears. "Come in."

Bryce unwrapped his sub and took a massive bite of it before Bella's form appeared in my doorway. When my office's soft lighting illuminated her curves, nothing else existed except her amber-brown eyes holding mine.

"I'm so sorry to interrupt, but one of your investors is downstairs, wanting to see you."

That caught Bryce's attention. "Wait, who's downstairs?"

Bella shrugged. "He said his name is Mr. Miles Blanchard."

I sighed. "Jesus."

Bryce set down his sub. "I can take care of him. Let me just—"

I held out my hand as I stood. "Miss Bella?"

"Yes?"

Her angelic voice washed over me like the warm waves of the ocean. "Go tell Mr. Blanchard that I'll be right down. And offer him some refreshments. You remember where the kitchen is?"

She blinked. "I believe so."

I nodded. "Offer something to eat or drink and get it for him if he takes you up on it. I'll be down in a second."

She shuffled on her feet. "Actually..."

I clenched my jaw. "Yes?"

She sighed. "I kind of told him I'd come back down with you."

I felt Bryce's prying eyes on me as I drew in a sobering breath. "Well, for future reference, you do not speak for me. Understood?"

She nodded. "Yes, sir. My apologies."

I stepped from around my desk. "I'll be right back, Bryce."

"Sure you don't want me to come with?"

I waved him off before I buttoned my suit jacket at my waist. "I got it, no worries. I'll be back soon. But don't eat my food, you hear me?"

Bryce snickered. "I hate pickles; you know this."

"Which is why I piled my sub high with them."

Bella giggled, and it almost made me smile. I had to bury it, though. I couldn't let her know how she affected me. Not until I figured out why she did this to me, at least. I mean, I'd come across many attractive women during my lifetime. Money, partial fame, and nice suits did that to a man. But, there was something in the way she looked at me—in the way she spoke to me—that struck a chord with my cold, hardened heart.

And it was something I couldn't let her figure out, lest she leverage it against me.

"Again, I'm so sorry, Mr. Remington. I didn't mean to overstep."

Bella's voice filled my ear as we stepped onto the elevator together. And after I pushed the button for the main floor, I clasped my hands in front of me.

"Just don't let it happen again," I said curtly.

And even though we both fell silent as we traveled down in the elevator, I felt overwhelmed by her perfume. Or body spray. Or whatever the fuck it was that she was wearing. It wrapped around me like a warm blanket and threatened to tug me into her orbit, just like her smile did.

I'm in so much fucking trouble.

Yet, the thought made me grin as the elevator doors opened. Revealing Mr. Blanchard's stubborn ass standing next to Bella's desk, perched like a hawk and waiting for us both.

3

Bella

Standing in that elevator with Wyatt was pure and utter torture. The feel of his body heat radiating out toward me made me want to turn in his direction. The cheeky grin he had creeping across his face gave me the urge to kiss him. I had to draw in slow, steady breaths just to keep my mind focused on the fact that I was still clocked in, which reminded me that he was my boss.

Get it together, Bella. Good lord.

Even out of the corner of my eye, though, I still appreciated how handsome Wyatt was. His dark features sat against sun-kissed skin, and his lean body fit well in a suit. The grin spreading across his cheeks thinned out his lips showcased a winning smile that I was sure had broken many hearts throughout the years. His confident shoulders rolled back as the elevator doors opened. I heard him draw in a deep breath, and the rise of his chest pulled my gaze toward his body. And I drew in a thick breath of his oaky, sensuous cologne.

The smell of it made me weak in my knees. Hell, *he* made me weak in my knees. But, when the doors finished sliding open, I snapped my head forward. I had to put on an assertive façade. I couldn't let my boss know I was so drawn to him physically. Yet, every time I went to take a step forward, the scent of his cologne forced me to stay rooted inside the elevator.

It wasn't until he stepped out and addressed the man at my desk that I followed in his footsteps.

"Mr. Blanchard! To what do I owe this pleasure?"

My eyes flicked down to Wyatt's ass again, and I chastised myself. It felt like my mind was spinning out of control. I tried to focus on myself and the fact that my phone was ringing, but despite his body falling away from my own, the scent of his cologne merely blossomed. It reminded me of a meadow full of wildflowers surrounded by a thick, dense forest.

Then, my bubble burst.

"Where-iz-sh-zz-sh-she?" my father slurred.

My eyes widened as my father's drunken voice hit my ears.

"Bella! Where's-zz-my-girl?"

I rushed up to his side. "Dad, what in the world are you doing?"

He glared at me. "You-nee-t-come-home."

He stumbled toward me, and I caught him in my arms before he started hiccupping. Mortified, I felt myself flushing with embarrassment from my toes to my nose. I didn't dare look around, though. I didn't dare gaze into the eyes of those watching my father in horror.

I'm going to lose my fucking job.

"Dad, where's Mom? How did you—?"

He pointed his finger at my chest. "No-talk-back. Juss-zz-get-in-th-car."

My eyes widened. "You drove? Are you absolutely insane?"

Tears prickled the back of my eyes as my father tried to speak. But, the more he said, the more slurred his words became.

"Dad, I'm calling you a cab. You have to go home so I can get back to—"

He leaned heavily against me. "Come-home-prinzzess. Mom-don't-cook-zz-oup-like-you."

I shoved him upright. "All right, let's go. Come on, out the door."

"Hey, what-are-y—Bella!"

I hissed into his ear, "This is my first day on the job. Do you want bills paid this month? Because if you do, you'll leave. Now."

Dad turned around and stumbled on his feet, so I jutted my arms out to catch him. And as we stood by the front door of a job I knew I wouldn't have much longer, my father glared at me.

"Dad, don't. Please, don't make a scene with my boss—"

He spat while he talked. "Don't. You. Dare. Talk. To. Me. That. Way."

At least he's enunciating now.

"Dad, I'm clocked in. I'm working. It's the middle of the day. You need to go home and sleep this off."

He glared at me. "Do. As. I. Say. Get. Outside. Now."

I cupped his cheeks and lowered my voice. "I know you're drunk, and I know you won't remember this, but forgive me anyway because I'm shoving you out that door and doing what I need to do to save my job. Got it?"

Confusion wafted over his features. "Wha-huh?"

But, before I could spin Dad around and shove him out the front door, Wyatt stepped up beside me. "May I be of assistance?"

Dear God, let me drop dead now. "No, sir. I've got it, I promise."

Dad's eyes widened. *"You?"*

I looked up at Wyatt as he clasped his hands behind his back. "Me?"

Dad pointed his trembling finger at Wyatt's face. "You-work-zz-for-him!?"

I slipped between the two men and put my hands on Dad's shoulders. "I'm begging you, just stop. Let me get you home—I'll make up the time after hours, Mr. Remington, I swear—and then we can—"

Dad lunged at Wyatt. "No-girl-of-mine-zz-workin-for-you!"

I furrowed my brow. "What?"

Wyatt took everything in stride, though. "Would you like to tour our facilities? Possibly see where your daughter is working now? Because I think once you see how well we'll be taking care of her, you won't hesitate to approve of her new position."

I balked. "First off, I don't need my father's permission for anything."

Dad hiccupped, and I cupped my hand over his mouth so he wouldn't fire back.

"And secondly, I'm sorry. Let me get him home, and when I come back, I'll stay later to make up the time. Is that okay?"

Wyatt didn't acknowledge me, though. Instead, he kept speaking with my father. "We've also got some refreshments in the kitchen. There's lemonade. Sodas. Water."

Dad started wavering on his feet. "Guezz-water-woul —hiccup!"

I cringed. "Let's just—"

Dad leaned toward Wyatt. "You-got-a-deal. Lead-th-way."

To my horror, Dad started wobbling and stumbling after Wyatt, trying to keep up the pace as my boss started giving my drunk-ass father a tour. I slowly looked over at the investor, still standing off to the side of my desk, and he was balking with the same shock that wafted through my body. The man's eyes turned back to me, and he shot me a nasty look. One I probably deserved for bringing the drama of my personal life into the office—on my first damn day of work.

Nevertheless, I hurried after my boss and my father as they walked down the hallway. Wyatt showed him where the restroom was and the kitchen. He was kind enough to retrieve a bottle of water for my father and stood there while he guzzled it back.

But then Wyatt turned to me. "Miss Bella, go make sure Mr. Blanchard doesn't need anything while he waits."

My eyes darted between the two men. "Sir, I think maybe I should take my father—"

"Now, please."

I swallowed hard. "Yes, sir."

I scurried out of the room and straightened my back before walking up to Mr. Blanchard. He didn't seem to be in a mood to talk, but I engaged him long enough to figure out that he wanted a hot mug of coffee. Great choice because I needed one myself.

However, when I backtracked into the kitchen, no one was in there.

"What the fuck?" I whispered.

I looked around for Wyatt and my father before I relegated myself to making a pot of coffee. I poured two fresh mugs before adding a bit of cream and sugar, then took the cups back out into the main lobby. I set one near my things before handing the other to Mr. Blanchard.

But, he didn't even take it from me. "Did I say I wanted cream and sugar?"

I prepared my words carefully. "My apologies, sir. It won't take me but a minute to whip up another—"

Wyatt appeared behind me. "I'm sure your coffee is simply wonderful, Miss Bella. Isn't that right, Mr. Blanchard?"

I looked up at him as the two men stared off with one another. And then reluctantly, the investor took the mug out of my hand.

"I'm sure it is," he mumbled.

Wyatt nodded. "Wonderful."

I lowered my voice. "Sir?"

He peeked down at me. "He's in the last room on the right down the hallway. I laid him down on a couch in there. He can sleep it off and catch a ride home with you once you clock out at your regular time. Okay?"

I nodded softly. "Oh-okay. Um, thank you."

His eyes whipped back to the investor. "Mr. Blanchard! Follow me. We'll have privacy in my office to speak."

"About time," the man murmured.

He shoved the untouched mug of coffee back into my hands, and I figured, hell, more for me to choke down. I watched the two men walk down the hallway and load onto the elevator. The second the doors closed, I chugged down the coffee. I growled and shook my head before returning the mug to the kitchen. And just for shits and giggles, I walked down the hallway to poke my head into the room where my father supposedly slept.

Right where Wyatt said he'd be.

Dad's soft snores filled the room, and I sighed. I reached for the door and closed it tightly, locking it from the inside out. That way, no one would burst in unexpectedly on him while he slept. Besides, the massive keyring I found in one of my desk drawers probably had a key that went to that room if I needed to get back in. Hopefully, at least.

As I sat back down at my desk, though, shock rolled over my body. I was stunned at Wyatt's treatment of my father and even more shocked at the fact that he was willing to let my father sleep it off here. The idea of my dad driving in that state horrified me, and I knew I'd chew Mom's ass off the second I got home. It was like raising two neglected, emotionally stunted toddlers, and I knew I'd be in for a knock-down, drag-out fight.

But for now, I relished in Wyatt's secretive side as I reached for my original mug of coffee. Because apparently, there was more than met the eye with that tall, dark, and devilish man.

❀ 4 ❀

Wyatt

I escorted Mr. Blanchard into my office—wondering where Bryce and my lunch had disappeared to—but I knew by the purse of his lips, I'd get an earful regarding Bella's father. Still, I felt for her. I'd witnessed my fair share of embarrassing parents of employees we had hired over the years, but none of them had been as difficult as that one. The idea that Bella was dealing with a drunk at home didn't sit well with me.

I made my way to my desk. "So, what can I do for you, Mr. Blanchard?"

He sat in front of it. "I don't believe I need to remind you that some of us on the board aren't very happy with the changes this company has been making."

Which is why we should be a family-run company. "I'm aware, yes."

"Have you given any thought as to why we're not happy?"

I eased myself into my chair. "Because the percentage of the company you own isn't bringing in the kind of money it used to?"

He blinked. "Well, yes."

I folded my hands in my lap. "I'm very well versed on why the board of investors, as a whole, isn't happy with the way things are going with the company right now. But, I guarantee you that if I pulled monetary schematics from every major company in this country during a state of growth for them, you'd see a loss in capital returns because of the money being reinvested into the company. Which is something you signed off on when you originally joined the board."

He leaned forward. "I know damn good and well what's in that contract. What I don't like is not getting a hard and fast date for when our earnings are going to start inching up due to all of this 'growth.'"

I shrugged. "Will and Bryce have told me we need at least another quarter."

"Another quarter? It's already been two since we started the refinery project."

I nodded. "You're correct, but the refinery only just got up and running two months ago. Surely, you can understand why that would affect the numbers."

He pointed at me. "Now, you listen here. You wouldn't

have a company if it were not for our financial backing. If everyone on the board dropped this company like a sack of potatoes, you guys would be—"

I crossed my leg over my knee. "Go on, be brave enough to finish that sentence."

Mr. Blanchard drew in a deep breath. "All I'm trying to say is—"

"—that you want things to go back to the way they were when you were siphoning money off a company you don't actively help with. Correct?"

"I don't enjoy being taunted or belittled, Wyatt."

I clicked my tongue. "And I don't enjoy someone completely ignorant about this company strolling in unannounced without an appointment just to tell me how he thinks things should be run because it benefits the few people in this company who don't do anything but cut checks, *Miles*."

He shook his head. "Where's Ryan? He's the more level-headed one of the bunch."

I stood to my feet. "Ryan is currently on paid leave for the next three months. Remember? He and Ellie have a new addition to their family."

He blinked. "Who's Ellie?"

I wanted to gouge the man's eyes out. "You can see yourself out the same way you came. And the next time you wish to meet with me, schedule an appointment with Miss Bella downstairs. She has my full schedule right on her computer."

He scoffed as he stood. "I knew this was a mistake. All of

it. The refinery. Moving the headquarters to this blank slate of a town. What is there to even do around here during conferences?"

I slid my hands into my pockets. "Oh, I don't know. Maybe you could come to the conferences and work now instead of bar hop."

His voice dropped. "Don't think I'm just here for my benefit. There are others on the board who aren't too happy with this little arrangement."

I shrugged. "And I knew I'd run into this issue when we were first tossing around plans. Rest assured, I have things set in motion to even the playing field and put everyone on the same page.

Once my family agrees to buy you fuckers out of this company for good.

Mr. Blanchard buttoned his suit jacket. "Then, I can't wait for those plans to come to fruition. Times are tough right now."

I snickered. "Times are tough for a man worth fifteen million? Somehow, I think not."

He shot me a look. "Have a good rest of your day, Mr. Remington."

I nodded. "And to you, Mr. Blanchard."

I watched him like a hawk as he left my office, then I fell back into my chair. I knew this wouldn't be the end of him, or the board, in general. It was why I hoped with all my might that the rest of the family would agree to buy out the board and make this company a family-owned operation. These men were killing me and bleeding us dry at the same time. They were vultures, all of them. And I wanted them gone.

For good, if I could finagle it.

Nevertheless, the anger wafting around inside my gut at the big-dick energy Miles fucking Blanchard just came in here with made me sick to my stomach. Who the hell did that man think he was, barging in here like that unannounced? If I knew I wouldn't have received such backlash from Bryce, I would have seen him out as quickly as he had slipped through those doors.

And the audacity of him to speak to Miss Bella like that.

Classless little newt.

The fact that the board existed wasn't the only issue, though. The broad-sweeping problem was the average age of our board. It made me so upset that there were people above us who owned the damn company who were our parents' age—and some of them quite a bit older—who thought they knew better about this company and its future. The average age of all our employees combined was under forty. Yet, an investor board with combined ages of five times that figure were making massive, far-reaching determinations on what we should do with a company in the modern times they seemed to disconnected from. At the very least, I wished for us to have one or two younger members on the board to help the older farts see things in a more progressive manner.

But, I knew that was only a Band-Aid on the actual wound that needed healing.

Or an infected, gangrenous sore that needing carving out altogether.

"Wait, have I sent that email?" I murmured.

I turned my attention to my computer and started typing away. I narrowed my eyes as I navigated to my "sent" folder, and I didn't see the outgoing email to my siblings. I cursed myself as I clicked on my "drafts" folder, and sitting there, waiting for me to proofread it, was the third round of an email I'd been crafting for over a month now.

The email that could change the course of this company for good.

My eyes scanned the document, and I started rewording a few things. I didn't want my anger and my frustration to come through in my verbiage. And every time I sat down to write this message, I was angrier than a hornet's nest in water. I titled the email "Urgent, Read Now," and I hoped that was enough to get everyone's attention.

Today's the day.

I edited the email one last time before I attached all of the pie charts and documents I'd been working on in my spare time. They spelled out everything from how much it would take to buy out the board, what we'd have to do contractually to circumvent their kickback, and how much we'd all be able to pocket over the first three years of this family outright owning our own damn petrol business, not just in title but in stocks and profit.

Then, after drawing in a sobering breath that sucked my

anger back down into the black pit of my soul, I pressed "send," hoping and praying my family had enough sense and money put aside to take on this venture.

They've all got growing families, though.

I leaned back in my chair and ran my finger across my lower lip. That would stunt things. It seemed that the men in the Remington family were finally getting broody enough to strike out and have families of their own. And with families came those houses they were building, which surely took a significant chunk of money out of their personal accounts. Whether or not we'd all have the money to pool together was an uncertain variable and one I hoped we didn't have to battle in order to make this a reality.

To be honest, I'd be willing to cover what they couldn't with my own fucking money for a slightly larger percentage. Anything to get us out of playing these dumbass business politics with a detached board of investors. They gave Bart too much of a runaround for my liking with the refinery in the first place. And to know some of them were pissed that our family business's headquarters was in the *family's* hometown drove it all home for me.

We needed these idiots out and quickly.

I closed out my email and flipped over to Ryan's, then chuckled when I saw the fact that he had already opened and read my email. I guessed he was already bored or needed something to take his mind off the chaos of everything he was juggling.

"And they call me a workaholic," I murmured.

But, a knock at my office door pulled me from my thoughts. And for once, I was thankful for the distraction.

"Come in," I called out only to raise my eyes and see Bella standing in the doorway with her father.

Bella

Dad groaned next to me. "Anyone got Tylenol?"

I whispered to him, "If you were home, you'd have some. You don't get that luxury here. Now, do what I told you."

I straightened my back as Wyatt stood from his desk.

"I have to admit, I thought you'd sleep more than that." Wyatt didn't move.

Dad grumbled something I didn't catch, so I nudged him.

"Now," I murmured.

Dad rolled his eyes. "I'm sorry for coming here in that... state."

Wyatt started digging around in his desk. "Well, you really

know how to spice up a workday." He walked over with two Tylenol in his outstretched hand, and Dad quickly took them.

"Got any water?" he asked.

I glared at him. "You're a big boy. Pop 'em and swallow."

Wyatt chuckled, and the sound wafted over me like a warm summer breeze. I looked up into his face and found him studying me intensely, and I wondered why. My knees went weak beneath his gaze as his eyes quickly swept down my body. And when Dad finally swallowed the two pills, I pulled myself out of my trance because the last thing I needed was him watching me stare at my damn boss.

He gets more handsome every time I see him.

Wyatt clapped his hands together, causing my father to jolt at my side. "Well, I'm glad to see you up and around. Feel more than free to help yourself to anything in the kitchen downstairs. There's plenty of water, plenty of snacks, and I'm sure you can find yourself with a full stomach before you head back home, Mr. Lancaster."

I nudged my father one last time, and he sighed. "I promise it won't happen again. Thank you for your generous hospitality."

Wyatt looked over at me. "Well-rehearsed, I see."

I blushed. "He wanted to come up here to see you."

Wyatt blinked. "I'm sure."

Dad didn't really do a good job of selling it, either. "Anyway, guess I should make my way home now. Bella, you still following me back like I'm a child?"

I glared at him. "When you stop acting like one, I'll stop treating you like one."

I turned my attention back to Wyatt and found him grinning, which didn't help the situation with my knees. "I haven't clocked out for lunch yet, so I'm clocked out now. I figured following him home would probably be met with a need for food, and I didn't want to do any of that on company time."

He nodded. "No worries, your job will be intact when you return."

I breathed a sigh of relief. "Wonderful. Okay. Dad, you ready?"

I watched him stare at Wyatt for another beat before he looked at me. "Yeah, I'm ready. But, this man better keep his hands off you. I see how he's looking at you."

I gawked. "Dad!"

Wyatt chuckled again. "Just a father protecting his daughter. If I had a daughter, I'd do much of the same."

I didn't know whether to be incredibly turned on or incredibly horrified, so I bid Wyatt a quick goodbye before dragging my father down the hallway by his arm. I was mortified, embarrassed, and, most of all, pissed. And all I wanted was for this damn day to be over so I could stuff my face with comfort food, put on my cozy pajamas, and have it out with my father inside of my head. Because I knew when I got home tonight, he'd be passed-out drunk again. Just like every other night for the past however many years.

"There gonna be soup or something when I get home?" Dad asked.

It took me a second to rein in my anger at the question as the elevator doors closed on us. "I don't know. Ask Mom. I have a job and a life outside of you two, so maybe you should ask your wife before you ask your daughter."

He paused. "What did I do to deserve your anger like this?"

I slowly looked at him. "Are you fucking kidding me right now?"

He pointed at me. "Hey, I might not have your respect, but I'm still your father."

"Yes, and I'm the only breadwinner in the family right now. You want money for your morning beers?"

He sucked air through his teeth. "You talk about my drinking like it's a problem. I can quit whenever I want."

I rolled my eyes. "Yeah, yeah. Heard all that before."

The elevator doors opened, and I stormed off. I didn't even wait for my father. I didn't want to deal with his intolerable bullshit a second longer. So, when we got to the front doors, I paused.

"Have Mom call me when you get home, okay?" I asked.

Dad turned to face me. "So, what happened to escorting me home?"

I shrugged. "I have a job. I can't just drop that job whenever you do something dumb. That's Mom's problem now. Call her if you need anything."

He scoffed. "Your mother's just as air-headed as the day I—"

Wyatt's voice sounded behind me. "Having troubles finding the way out?"

I jumped at the intrusion and whipped around to find him perched against my desk with his arms crossed over his chest.

And his eyes drilled into my father.

"*Sir?*"

Dad growled beneath his breath. "This is a family issue, thanks."

I hissed at him. "Are you insane? That's my boss."

Dad shot me a look. "If you only knew what I know."

What the hell does that mean?

A man came through the front doors donning an impeccable black suit. "Mr. Lancaster?"

I furrowed my brow as Dad turned around. "And who the hell are you?"

The man stuck out his hand. "You can call me, Mr. Deleeay, sir. I'm employed with the company as a driver."

My father shook the man's hand curtly. "Great. Nice to meet ya."

"I'm here to take you home."

I peeked back over at Wyatt and found him grinning at the scene unfolding.

"No, thanks. Got my own car," Dad said.

I paused. "Actually, we'll take you up on that offer."

Dad's eyes found mine quickly. "Seriously, I don't need a damn driver. Just like I don't need someone escorting me home."

I quirked an eyebrow. "Like you also didn't need a nap to

sleep things off? Because I'm sure that's what you told Wyatt."

And his growing chuckle behind me told me that I was right.

"Look, Mr. Lancaster," Wyatt said as he walked over to us, "all I want to do is make this as painless as possible. There are a lot of things that need to get done today, and distractions always drag us behind."

Dad scoffed. "Of course, you and your selfish family would find my family to be an inconvenience."

I gasped. "Dad!"

Wyatt nodded, but I saw his jaw clench. "At any rate, if you go outside, you'll see Mr. Deleeay standing beside a very comfortable Town Car. Just climb into the back seat and enjoy the ride home. I'm sure there's even some sparkling water in there for you to enjoy."

Dad snickered. "I'm not an idiot. I'm sure I can find some guy standing by some car out there."

Wyatt nodded. "Well, everyone is prone to doing stupid things every once in a while. Just want to make sure we don't make the same mistake twice in one day."

I could have sworn my jaw was swinging against the floor. Watching these two men go toe to toe with one another frightened me in ways I didn't think possible. My father and my boss stared at one another as they both tried to tug me in different directions. I wasn't sure how I felt about it, but I did know one thing. Seeing Wyatt come to my defense did nothing for my growing crush on him.

I found my boss powerful and intimidating. But, there was clearly a soft side to him with how he treated my father earlier in the day. I mean, letting him sleep off some drunken stupor right here in a shared workspace? That took some serious empathy.

However, empathy wasn't currently etched across his face. If I read him correctly, frustration was written on his face.

"Dad?" I asked.

He turned to face me. "Yes, princess?"

I cherished the nickname. "You really need to go, okay? It's important to me."

His face softened. "All right, then I'll leave. But, don't you let someone like him push you around. If you need anything at all, I'm only a phone call away."

I kissed his cheek softly. "I know, Daddy. Thank you."

Wyatt drew in a deep breath. "And I'll make sure to it that the car you drove here gets home safely this evening. I'll have Mr. Deleeay drive it himself after Miss Bella clocks out."

Dad nodded curtly. "Great. Thanks."

After practically shoving my father out the front door, I let out the breath I had been holding. I leaned against the black doorway and closed my eyes, allowing myself just a second of peace and quiet. What a tumultuous first day I'd had, and it was only two in the afternoon.

"When you're finished," Wyatt said as he turned around, "come to my office. We need to talk."

I didn't turn to face him, but I watched his reflection fall away in the glass doors that slowly closed my father out of this place. I watched him walk down the hallway, not even peeking over his shoulder as he stepped onto the elevator. I swallowed hard as a knot formed in my stomach. He had just told me that my job was intact, right?

So, what did we need to speak about?

Probably nothing good.

I stole a few more moments to myself before I rushed over to my ringing phone. I had a few calls waiting for me, and I used my booklet to transfer them to the right offices before I disconnected my headset. I punched the button that turned on my automatic voice message box to answer any call that came in while I was away, then I headed for the elevator.

I ventured toward my boss's sprawling office to talk about whatever the hell it was he wanted to chew me out for.

Who knows, maybe this is a good thing.

I wrung my hands as I ascended back to the top of the building for the umpteenth time that day. I had a feeling I'd be spending more of my time up here anyway than down there, and I found my eyes gravitating toward the empty desk in the lobby right as I stepped off the elevator. I hadn't noticed it before, but after my father's outburst, I found myself salivating over it.

If I were up here, not only would I see Wyatt more, but it would be harder for my father to navigate this place and find me.

Then again, if he can't find me, he'd just kick up a stink until I did.

"Come on in, Miss Bella."

His voice wafted just beyond the door as I raised my fist

to knock against it. I paused and closed my eyes, giving myself one more second to settle my swirling stomach. Then, I eased the door open and slipped into his office.

"Close the door," he said.

And when I felt it shut behind me, Wyatt's eyes snapped to mine.

❧ 6 ❧

Wyatt

I held her gaze as I ushered her to sit in front of my desk. Then, I fluffed out my suit coat and perched on the edge of it. I watched as her thick hips swayed with every step she took. The way her wisps of unstrapped hair fluttered effortlessly around her face drew my eyes to her freckles. Every time she blushed, they grew darker. Every time she wrinkled that cute little nose of hers, they danced. And every time she smiled, they ignited with life.

I found myself wanting to kiss every single one of them.

"Yes, sir?" she asked softly.

My eyes danced around her face. "Is this going to be a regular thing with your father?"

She looked up at me, and her doe eyes stopped my heart in my chest. "No, sir. I can promise you that."

I narrowed my eyes. "You're sure that's a promise you can make?"

Her eye twitched. "My father, he's—"

I threaded my hands together and settled them against my thigh. "Take your time. Part of being employed here is understanding that we're all a family. You don't have to tell me anything you're not prepared to, but if I know more about the situation, I can better help you handle it if it *does* happen again."

She drew in a deep breath through her nose. "Back when I was little, my father was a massive rodeo racer. He tried just about all of it before he found his niche in steer wrestling. And when I was young—maybe ten or so—my father was in this parade they had scheduled for the little kids to watch."

Holy shit, no wonder the man looked familiar. "I know them. The ones where the racers come out and wave to the crowd and stuff."

"Exactly. One of those. Mom and I were right down there in the thick of it, and I was waving at him. Then, all of a sudden, Dad was on the ground underneath his horse. It happened so quickly that I didn't even catch what happened. In one moment, he was waving and smiling, and the next moment, Mom was hopping the fence to go help Dad, while everyone else trotted around him like nothing had happened."

"I'm sorry for what happened to him."

She leaned back in the chair. "He wasn't the same after

that. The force of the fall broke all of his ribs at once. He needed extensive surgery on his back. He's in chronic pain, hence the drinking. And of course, it took away the one thing he did for a living."

"Which would be hard on anyone, much less a man who provides for his family."

She nodded slowly. "It's been a hard road for all of us. My going off to college was rough, especially on Mom. My father is why she can't work. Every time she took a job, he'd pull this same kind of shit—I mean stuff—and he'd get her fired."

I chuckled. "No need to edit ourselves when it's just us. Out at your desk? Yes. But, in my office? You can let them fly."

She smiled, and it gripped my blackened soul. "I appreciate that."

"So, now you're working a job you probably didn't see for your future because you need to take care of your family."

"Correct, and I promise you I'm going to do whatever it takes, so there isn't another episode like that."

I leaned forward. "Well, allow me to be the first to say that if it does happen again, you aren't going to get fired."

What I didn't think was appropriate to tell her was the fact that I understood. I knew what she was going through. I remembered that day so vividly in my mind that I didn't think I'd ever get rid of the memory. All of us were at that same rodeo. Dad and the rest of the competitors, trotting around on their horses and waving at the crowd. Shooting T-shirts into the stadium and helping to raffle off free drinks and shit like that.

What Bella didn't know was that I knew what took her father down. I knew why her father had hit the ground and had his horse topple on top of him. I knew who was responsible, too.

I just didn't know if it was my place to tell her because the story she remembers wasn't the reality of what had happened.

Bella's voice tore me from the recesses of my mind. "From the bottom of my heart, thank you so much for being so understanding about this. Honestly."

I stood to my feet. "Now that we have that nasty business out of the way, I can speak on something a bit more uplifting."

"Oh? What about?"

I grinned. "It's commonplace for new employees to be taken out to dinner after their first day. So, I'll stop by your desk promptly at five to pick you up."

Bella blinked. "Pick me up... for dinner?"

I walked back around behind my desk. "Yes. It's the least you deserve for being such a strong crux for your family, and then we get to go out somewhere nice on behalf of the company's credit card."

"Wait, I'm sorry. Did you just ask me out to dinner?"

I smirked. "Yes but a business dinner. It's simply something we do here, but if it makes you uncomfortable, we don't have t—"

She stood to her feet. "No, no, no! It's fine."

I smiled at her hastiness before she cleared her throat.

"I mean, I was just—a bit caught off guard. That's all."

I sat down in my chair. "Understood. People have told me I pivot a bit too quick sometimes."

She giggled. "I can see why."

The sound made my cock stiffen. "I'll see you at five then, Miss Bella."

She thumbed over her shoulder. "So, I'm dismissed?"

My eyes locked with my computer screen. "Yes, ma'am. You are dismissed."

I was lying through my teeth, of course. I wanted to be around her, no matter the means I had to go to in order to make it happen. But, part of me also felt guilty. That rodeo accident fifteen years ago didn't just take out her father. It took out my father, too. He hadn't so much as mounted a horse ever since that day but not because he had gotten injured. But because his guilt was too great.

I'm sorry for what my father did to yours, Bella.

And I hoped this dinner was the first step in mending fences between our families that had been broken for far too long.

A quick knock came at my door. "I'm sorry, Wyatt, but the elevator isn't working, I don't think?"

I looked up at the sound of Bella's voice. "Ah, it must be jammed again. We've been having some trouble with it. Here, I'll come out and see what I can do."

She shook her head. "No, no, that's totally okay. I just can't find the stai—"

I stood from my desk and ignored her plea as I slid past her at the door. I waited in the hallway and held out my hand, escorting her back toward the elevator. I placed my hand on the small of her back, gauging her response as my palm touched her clothing.

And when we stopped, I could've sworn I felt her lean into my touch. I grinned as I balled up my free fist. "All right, let's give this a go."

I slammed my fist against the button, and it lit up before the doors slid open. Bella giggled as she shook her head, and I grinned down at her as she walked into the elevator.

"I guess I'll see you soon then, *Fonz.*"

A genuine smile crossed my face. "I'm looking forward to it."

I waited for the doors to close, then counted to ten just to make sure she didn't have yet another reason to backtrack. And once I knew she wasn't coming back up here for something else, I slid my hand into my pants.

"Fucking penis won't go down," I murmured to myself.

I situated my half-erect cock against my body before breathing a sigh of relief. I didn't know what kind of hold this woman had over me, but I hoped to figure it out over dinner. I walked back into my office and closed the door, and dammit if her fucking perfume wasn't still lingering at the entrance. I leaned against the door and closed my eyes. I inhaled the glorious scent and felt the heat of the small of her back still etching itself against my palm.

And as my cock grew thicker, I second-guessed my decision for dinner tonight.

Can I even make it through a damn meal?

"Of course, I can. I'm Wyatt fucking Remington," I murmured.

After drawing in a few deep breaths, I felt my cock dwindling to its original size. And after I was sure my erection was gone, I thrust myself back into work. I incessantly checked my email, wondering if any of my brothers had replied to it, and grew frustrated at the lack of responses.

Still, for men with families, it was a choice they surely needed to talk over with their counterparts. But then, why the hell hadn't Boone responded?

Someone's got a secret.

Either that, or he was being a lazy ass.

Nevertheless, the deeper I dug into work, the quicker time flew by. And when my alarm went off at five minutes to five, I quickly packed away my things. I slid folders into my briefcase that I'd take home and work on tonight with mindless television in the background; then, I headed straight for the stairs.

I bounded down them, trying to work off some of my needless energy before I burst through the doors and eyed Bella's desk.

Time for dinner, beautiful.

7

Bella

"Ready?"

I peeked over my shoulder and saw Wyatt standing there with a grin on his face. He clutched his briefcase in his left hand and had his right hand slid into the pocket of his suit pants.

"Ma'am?" the woman on the line asked.

Her voice snapped me from my trance, and I pressed the "send" button on the email I was typing up. "Yes! My apologies. I just sent your confirmation email. I can hold until you receive it."

Wyatt chuckled, and the sound prickled the hairs on the nape of my neck.

"Got it! Thank you so much, Bella."

I smiled. "My pleasure. I hope you have a wonderful rest of your evening."

"You, too!"

Wyatt's voice appeared again. "Cordial and peppy. I like it."

I snickered. "Let me just log out, and I'll be ready to go."

I quickly gathered my things and shut down my station after my first dizzying day of work. Then, Wyatt escorted me through the front doors. I noticed he didn't lock them as we left, and I wondered if that meant he'd be coming back to get more work done after we finished with food.

I won't keep him too long, then.

I started veering over toward my car before I felt his hand against the small of my back, and it held me in its warm trance so much that I didn't even notice where we headed until Wyatt opened a truck door for me. I blinked and looked around, watching my car from the other side of the parking lot.

"You sure you don't want me to drive? I can just follow you," I said.

Wyatt offered me his hand. "Nonsense. It doesn't make sense to take two vehicles to the same place. I'll simply bring you back to your car once we're finished. I have work I need to tend to this evening anyway."

I took his hand. "Then, I won't keep you long."

He chuckled. "You take however long you wish. This is your celebratory dinner."

The feeling of my hand against his alleviated all too soon.

Then, he climbed into his truck, and away we went. However, as we started passing all of Conroe's restaurants, I furrowed my brow when I saw the "leaving city limits" sign off in the distance.

"Where are we headed?" I asked.

Wyatt leaned back in his seat. "A little place off the beaten path that doesn't get as much recognition as it should. Plus, the view of the town from the balcony is outstanding."

The farther we pulled away from the city limits, the more I saw Wyatt relax. And by the time we pulled into the hillside restaurant with a porch that boasted of extraordinary scenic views, my boss practically had his back slouched and his legs spread while driving. It was the most relaxed I'd seen him, and I had to admit my eyes were drawn to him.

That was until he cut the engine to his truck. "Ready?"

I blinked rapidly and tossed my focus down to my purse. "Ready when you are."

"Great. I'll come around and get you."

He was a gentleman the entire way in. He helped me out of his truck and offered me his arm. He escorted me inside and even pulled out my chair once we got out to the balcony. Wyatt then poured my glass of wine, doting on me like I was a fucking queen.

And I loved it.

"To your employment," Wyatt said. He held up his glass, so I did the same.

"To my employment, and my keeping this job despite my father's bullshit."

He chuckled. "Here, here to that."

We clinked our glasses together, and I watched him peer at me from beyond the rim of the crystal. I started feeling nervous, so I panned my gaze out toward the horizon. Conroe twinkled in this little valley it was nestled in, and the heavy night sky that hung over us was unimpeded by lights.

It was the most beautiful thing I'd ever seen.

"Orion's out tonight," Wyatt said.

I whipped my gaze to him. "Huh?"

He pointed. "That cluster of stars? Connected by those? That's Orion's Belt. You can really see it tonight without the clouds in the sky."

I furrowed my brow. "You know about constellations?"

He shrugged. "Call it a hobby."

What else don't I know about you? "How long have you enjoyed them?"

"What? Constellations?"

I nodded. "Mhm. When did you get interested in astronomy?"

He shrugged. "When I was a teenager."

"What spurred it on?"

"Boredom."

So, we're back to the clipped sentences. "Sometimes, I like to believe that astrology and things like that are real."

He chuckled. "I don't put much stock into it."

I nodded slowly. "Ah."

He was the most confusing person on the planet. One second, he was relaxed and opening up. And the next, it was as if someone had slammed a prison door in his face and locked him away from the rest of the world. He was an enigma that I couldn't figure out. But, after the waiter came and took our order, he seemed to open up a bit more.

Then again, it could have been the second glass of wine we had downed together.

"You're going to love the surf and turf. It's incredible here," Wyatt said.

I smiled. "When I don't know what to choose, why not have both?"

He snickered. "Don't say that to Boone. You'll give him ideas."

I quirked an eyebrow. "Boone?"

He set down his wine glass. "My younger brother. He's pretty much a man-whore. Will was, too. My half-brother. But, he has since reformed his ways and become a family man."

I almost spat out my wine. "Oh, my God. Warn me next time, would ya?"

He barked with laughter. "Now, where's the fun in that?"

I leaned back in my seat. "Do you want to be a family man someday?"

I watched his eyes gaze out toward the outline of Conroe, and I saw something flicker behind his stare. I wasn't sure what it was, mostly because I didn't know if the wine was playing tricks on me or not. But, I could have sworn I saw regret wash over his features for a moment.

As quickly as it had risen, though, it vanished. And Wyatt

threw back the rest of his wine before setting it back onto the table.

"You know, I usually don't drink during the week," Wyatt said.

I watched him reach for his water as our waiter came out with our food. I turned that little tidbit of information over in my head as dish after dish kept coming out. Why was he drinking now if he didn't drink during the week? Was I that hard on him?

Back off, Bella. You're coming on too strong.

"Why don't you drink during the week?" I asked.

He picked up his fork. "Just not something I usually do. I have a tendency to slip whenever I'm around my brothers, seeing as 'beer o'clock' apparently means 'anytime they want to get drunk.' I like to uphold a more professional demeanor, however, due to the nature of our company."

"So, why are you drinking now?"

He grinned. "I can get away with a bit more up here. That's why I like it."

"Because it's secluded and no one can find you?"

His eyes locked with mine. "Precisely."

I felt a shiver of warmth ricochet down my body until it found its home between my legs. My cheeks flushed a bright red that I felt aching my skin, so I looked down at my food. There was so much on my plate that I knew I'd end up taking at least half of it home, if not more. But, that didn't stop me from picking up my fork and eating as much as I could.

While we ate, things were pretty silent. But, once we both

got to-go boxes to take our leftovers with us, Wyatt's voice hit my ears.

"If I made you feel bad for having wine, that isn't what I meant to do."

And for the second time that day, I saw a compassionate and empathetic side to this hardened man that I hadn't expected to witness.

"No, no. It's okay. As weird as it sounds, I drink before my food gets here. When I'm actually eating, I don't like the taste of drinks impeding on the taste of the food."

He smirked. "A woman after my own heart."

My gut clenched. My heart stopped in my chest. The way he was staring at me made me feel vulnerable and beautiful. I enjoyed the way he looked at me. Dare I say, I even loved it.

Holy shit, I'm in so much trouble.

I drew in a short breath of air through my nose. "So, what do you do when you're not working?"

He leaned back. "I don't have many moments in my life when I'm not. But, on the off chance when they do happen, I enjoy being outside. Camping. Riding horses."

"Do you compete like your family?"

His eyes grew dark. "No."

All right, staying away from that subject. "I think that's great. After what happened to my father, I can't bring myself to get interested in rodeos any longer. They're so dangerous, and people just sit there and cheer it on like it's nothing."

I expected him to say something, but he didn't. Instead, he kept staring at me, like there was something on my face. I picked up my napkin and, as lovingly as I could, dabbed and wiped at my lips and my cheeks. Maybe I did have something on my face. Perhaps I had missed a crumb or a dribble of something. Or, he could be staring at me for a different reason altogether.

"Tell me something about you that I don't know," Wyatt said.

I put my napkin back in my lap. "Well, I went to college for—"

He waved his hand in the air. "Tell me something I can't find in your employee records."

I blinked. "I'm not sure I'm following."

He leaned forward. "I want to know a secret. Something that you rarely entrust to people."

I furrowed my brow. "Why?"

He leaned back again, looking as collected as a wolf in waiting. "Because I don't readily tell many people I come across that I'm not into the rodeo scene like the rest of my family. It's only fair that you level the playing field, yes?"

I mean, I could tell him...

I fought myself on it for a while and decided against it. I mean, why the hell did I even consider telling the man I was a virgin? After all, it would only put him off me. Men like Wyatt wanted a woman who knew what she wanted. Who knew what she enjoyed. Who knew what she was good at. No one wanted a twenty-five-year-old who hadn't even had sex yet. That was preposterous!

So, I buried that particular secret and decided on another one.

"All right then," I said as I reached for my water, "a secret for a secret."

Wyatt patiently waited as I sipped my water, turning over how to phrase it in my mind. Then, my eyes rose to his.

"My father has been an alcoholic for so long that, even after pursuing my dreams in college, I'd have to come home and take care of my parents. And some days, like today, I know I could look my father in his eyes and tell him that I hate him."

Nothing like a good, vengeful hate to crush whatever it is that's brewing between my boss and me.

It was probably for the best, anyway. Especially considering the fact that I needed this job.

8

Wyatt

I kept my cool on the outside, but on the inside, I was fuming. I wanted nothing more than to slap some sense into her father and tell him to wake the fuck up. Everyone went through tragedy. Everyone went through something significant in their lives. And it didn't give Bella's father the right to do what he was doing to her. I saw the sincerity in her eyes but also the guilt. And I had nothing but sympathy for her. All I wanted was to take her into my arms, hold her close, and let her know that things would be all right.

But, I settled for my words instead. "I'll say it as many times as necessary. Your job won't disappear because of your father's antics."

Bella nodded softly. "I appreciate it."

I shrugged. "No need. It wouldn't be fair for you to lose your job over the actions of your father. You shouldn't have to pay some high price for a grown man's problems."

And when she smiled, I felt hope blossom in my chest.

I enjoyed how I felt with Bella, even if I wasn't used to it. She made me feel... important. As if I hadn't been glossed over in life. Don't get me wrong; I enjoyed coming from a large family. But sometimes, I got drowned out in the hustle and bustle of drinking and joking around when we needed to buckle down and get shit done. I was the butt of most family jokes, especially around the holidays. They always teased me about constantly working and not being able to let loose.

But what they didn't know was that I worked to get away from their teasing in the first place.

I felt like a person with Bella, not just a worker. I actually felt seen with her, not just looked at. I felt as if I were heard, not simply listened to. And I enjoyed that immensely. However, I knew it wasn't the kind of feeling that was conducive to a professional relationship. So, despite finagling things to get her out here with me, I figured it was time for reality to creep back into the situation, which made me stand to my feet.

Time to go home before things get worse. "Ready to head out?"

Bella stood in kind. "Ready whenever you are."

I offered her my arm. "Come. I'll walk you out."

We made our way back out to my truck, and Bella sat a little closer to me than she had on the ride over. I kept peeking at her, watching as she shifted around, only to end up a little nearer every single time. And even though I steeled myself and doubled-down on guarding my needs, I enjoyed it.

No, I didn't enjoy it.

I adored it.

The closer she got, the more her heat radiated toward me. It felt like her aura was actively reaching out toward mine, and all I had to do was cave for my wishes to come true. I shivered internally at the thought.

Yet, when I felt Bella's arm brush against mine, it reminded me of just how close she'd gotten. And how I couldn't like it as much as I did.

I pulled into the parking lot and parked in my usual spot. At least parking far away from Bella's car would give me one last chance to feel her arm wrapped around my own. I turned off the engine and hopped down, jogging around so I could offer my hand as she touched down onto the asphalt.

But, when she got out of my truck, she didn't relinquish my hand. "Thank you for dinner, Wyatt. I had a really nice time."

I gazed down into her eyes and felt a grin spread across my face. My lips didn't move, though. I was afraid that if I opened them, my true intentions would come shooting out before I could swallow them down. The twinkling stars above our heads reflected in her eyes, though. Streetlamps flickered on in the distance, casting a glow across our bodies. A full moon hung heavily in the sky, pregnant with the whispers of what might be.

Even *I* had to admit it was a wonderful night to take chances.

Without another word spoken, I wrapped her arm around my own. I walked her back to her car, feeling her leaning against me as if she needed support. I resisted the urge to put my arm around her waist, though I very much wanted to feel her voluptuous curves against my body. However, once we got to Bella's car, I saw upfront—and firsthand—just how beat up that rust bucket was.

Literally. Rust on the bottom was eating away at the metal frame. She had a donut on the back left tire that looked like it hadn't been changed out in weeks. Hell, the damn front driver-side tire looked a bit flat. And all of her fucking tires were practically bald.

It's an accident waiting to happen.

I didn't like it, either.

"Well, I suppose the good news is that the paperwork for your company vehicle should go through by the end of the week."

Bella ripped away from me and turned on a dime as her jaw hit the floor. "Wait. What?"

I slid my hands into my pockets and turned to face her. "What, what?"

She furrowed her brow tightly. "There was nothing in my contract that said anything about a company vehicle."

I shrugged. "Doesn't have to be. Company policy dictates that the head of every department gets one, no questions asked."

She blinked. "But I'm just a secretary?"

"No, you're not. You're the head of our secretaries. You're in charge of coordinating them and making sure they stay on task and ensuring everyone has everything together and populated into one system we can all access. So, you get a company car."

Her eyes watered. "That's—thank you, Wyatt. I mean, Mr. Remington. I just—thank you so much."

I chuckled. "Again, no need to thank me. It's simply company policy."

My heart melted at her gratitude, and when that beautiful smile crossed her face, I hoped to be able to make her smile like that every single damn day. Out of nowhere, though, she lurched at me, wrapping her arms around my neck as tightly as she could.

And when I felt her curves pressed against my body, I had to swallow back a growl.

"Thank you so much," she whispered against the shell of my ear.

The heat of her breath was my ending blow. I couldn't contain myself a second longer. I slid my arms around her waist, holding her close against me as I buried my face into the crook of her neck. The sigh that left her lips stiffened my cock. My lips puckered against her skin. And when she moaned softly, I sucked a patch of skin between my teeth before picking her up off her feet.

"Should we be doing this?" she asked breathlessly.

I kissed her neck again. "I don't fucking care."

She slid her fingers through my hair. "Me, neither."

"Good."

I walked her back over to my truck and reached out for the handle. I flipped the tailgate down and sat her against it, allowing my hands to massage up and down her thighs. I pulled back, taking in the valley of her breasts as she cupped my cheeks. And when my eyes lifted to hers, my hand flew into her hair, gripping it before I pulled her lips down to my own.

The sensation washed over me like bubbles in a tub. I felt dragged beneath her current as it tugged me out into a bubbling sea of satisfaction. Her arms tightened around my neck. My head fell off to the side, deepening the kiss as my tongue ravished the roof of her mouth. She locked her legs around me, rolling that heated pussy against my stomach. And all I could think about was how deeply I wanted to bury my cock between her legs.

"Lean back," I commanded against her lips.

She lowered herself to the bed of my truck, and I climbed up. I crawled over her, wrapping my hand behind her back before I effortlessly eased her farther up. She squealed with delight and locked her body around me, clinging tightly as the scent of her womanhood wafted up my nostrils. I growled as I kissed her clothed tits. I settled her back against the floor before I reached up, unlatching the metal container I had permanently situated just beyond my reach.

And when I flipped up the lid, out popped a sheer covered top that shielded us from the rest of the world.

While still giving us a beautiful view of the nighttime sky.

Bella giggled. "You do this often?"

I reached for a pillow and eased it beneath her head. "No."

She cocked her head. "What's the sheer shield for, then? What do you use it for?"

I tucked a loose strand of hair behind her ear. "Cover while fishing. Just kind of back my truck up and go from there."

"Ah, you're a fisherman."

I pressed her legs open with my knees. "Yep."

She giggled. "I've never been fishing."

I pinned her wrists above her head. "It's boring."

She barked with laughter. "Then, why do you fish?"

I pulled out a blanket and covered our bodies with it. "Gives me something to talk about with my brothers."

I wasn't sure what rushed behind her eyes, but I didn't care. All I cared about was invading Bella's body until we both cried out for mercy.

So, I crashed my lips down against hers and felt her buck against me, her body begging me to infiltrate.

9

Bella

His kiss robbed me of my breath, and everything else fell to the wayside. He blanketed my body away from the rest of the world as his tongue slid across mine. I was doing the unthinkable and on my first day at my job to boot! But, I couldn't deny the warmth spreading throughout my veins with every brush of his tongue against my mouth.

And I pressed on with a roll of my hips.

I felt his growing cock pushing against his pants, and it made me eager to touch him. My legs spread farther, giving my damp pussy some room to breathe before his knee edged against my wet panties. I bucked into him, wanting friction more than ever before. And as he kissed down my neck, his teeth slid against my pulse point.

Causing me to groan out his name. "Oh, Wyatt."

He growled. "That's it, Bella. Let it out."

His voice shivered me to my core. My nipples puckered against my bra as his hands kept my wrists pinned above me. I felt vulnerable and beautiful at the same time. I felt as if I were on top of the world, situated beneath his body. And when he finally relinquished my wrists, I thought maybe he had come to his senses. I thought perhaps he'd put a stop to all of this.

But, all he did was flip my dress up over my hips.

"Fucking hell, you're beautiful," Wyatt hissed.

I watched as he pulled out his cock, stroking it for me to behold. And the girth of the dick made my eyes widen while veins bulged from every angle. I'd never seen anything so beautiful in all my life, and he was already leaking from his tip.

Wyatt grinned at me as his hand disappeared between my legs. Then, he pulled my panties off to the side. In one fell swoop, he plunged into my depths, falling back down to my body. The pain and pleasure washed over me as I felt myself catapulted into the clouds. Finally, I knew what it felt like. Finally, I knew what everyone was talking about. And as he bottomed out against me, I felt his tightly wound curls tickling my swollen clit.

Take all of me, Wyatt.

His hands caught himself against the bed of the truck as

my jaw unhinged in silent pleasure. He staked my body against his, pinning me beneath him with the strength of his cock alone. And when he pinned my wrists back over my head, I knew I was at his mercy.

Then, he started pounding away.

"Oh, shit," I whispered.

He growled. "Fucking hell. So tight for me. Holy God, Bella."

My back arched. "Yes. Just like that. Oh, Wyatt. Don't stop. It's so—this is—"

It was like nothing else I'd ever experienced. Something tightened in my gut while my body bounced with every thrust. Wyatt hovered over me, his eyes caressing me as my juices dripped down my ass crack. And the deeper he slid into my body, the more he spread me.

Then, it was as if he propelled my body into the heavens. "That's it," I whimpered.

He captured my lips. "Come for me, Bella. Do it."

I bucked ravenously against him, meeting him thrust for thrust. "Yes. Yes. Yes. Wyatt, yes!"

He growled. "That's it, beautiful. Squeeze that dick."

I fell over the edge as my spine arched so tightly I thought it might shatter into pieces. My eyes rolled back, fuzzing out the stars and spiraling me into a darkness from which I never wanted to return. I was overwhelmed by him in the best of ways. His dick throbbed against my aching walls, and when his movements began to stutter, I knew he was close.

"Fall over with me," I gasped. And my words were all Wyatt needed.

"Holy shit, Bella. Never had a pussy this tight. Oh, yeah. Holy fuck. Ugh, shit."

When he collapsed against me, his hands released my wrists. And it gave me the opportunity to hold him. I wrapped my arms around his back, rubbing my hands up and down his spine as he panted against the crook of my neck. Our intermingled fluids dripped from between my thighs, and his cock slowly dwindled until it slid from its warm little home. And when I kissed the shell of his ear, I let myself revel in the smell of the two of us intertwined.

Before he pushed himself up and tucked his cock back into his pants. "Well, what a dessert," he said breathlessly

I laid there with my legs still spread as I gazed up at the stars. A hazy sort of pleasure blanketed my mind, but even I knew what was about to happen. We wouldn't cuddle like in the movies. We wouldn't kiss or go for another round. That was nothing but a hookup to Wyatt, yet it had been so much more for me.

Don't say anything. You're only going to freak him out.

"Bella?"

I willed my legs to close, which moved my panties back into their proper place. With the world still tilting around me, I forced myself upright, gazing at Wyatt as he stood in the parking lot. At some point in time, he had gotten off the back of the truck and was staring at me as if I had lost my damn mind.

Gone was the hazy pleasure in his eyes, and it had been replaced with something akin to regret. It made me feel cheap, and all I wanted was to get out of there.

"Yes, sorry. Just regaining my sea legs," I said with a small giggle.

He chuckled. "Glad I could make you feel that way."

Sorry, you don't. "Anyway, I guess I should be going."

He offered me his hand. "Here. I'll walk you back to your car."

I slid off the bed of his truck without his help. "No, no. It's okay. I'm just right over there."

His hand fell back to his side. "The parking lot is dark right now. At least let me—"

I started quickly walking away from him. "Thank you so much for a wonderful evening! I appreciate it!"

"Bella, wait!"

I walked away as quickly as I could without seeming hasty. But, I wasn't sure if I accomplished that last part. All I knew was that I had to leave before something else happened. Before I said something wrong or did something to permanently alter whatever the hell it was that I had with Wyatt. After all, it didn't make any sense for me to stay at a job if I couldn't even get along with my boss. And his promise not to relieve me of my position simply because of my father was a promise I wanted to capitalize on to the fullest extent.

Which meant not ruining my working relationship with my damn boss.

I heard Wyatt's footsteps following behind me and quickly

slipped into my car. I struck up the engine and backed out, then decided to wrap around the back of the building. I got away just in time for Wyatt to recede in my rearview mirror, but I didn't bother studying the look on his face.

I didn't want to see one of disappointment after memorizing one of utter ecstasy.

"I'm sorry," I whispered.

As I made my way home, tears sprang to my eyes. At least our clothes hadn't come off. That really made for my quick getaway. Plus, I wasn't sure if I wanted Wyatt to see my body in the first place. Not that I had confidence issues, I knew I rocked my curves with grace and poise. But, I always wanted the first time a man saw me naked to be like in the movies, where he couldn't stop staring at me, where his jaw dropped open, where he professed his undying need to worship me while kissing every inch of my body.

I wanted that moment.

And I now knew that Wyatt couldn't give that to me.

At least I still have a first for someone.

I brushed away my tears as I pulled into the driveway. And even though I saw my father peeking out through the curtains to see what was going on, I gave myself a moment to gather my thoughts. Sex wasn't at all what I thought it would've been like. I mean, it felt good, sure. But, I always thought there was cuddling or something after. Some sort of reassurance that what we had done wasn't one massive regret. That was all I felt, though—regret. I wanted to feel beautiful with Wyatt, but instead, I felt cheap. I wanted to feel on top of the world, but instead, I felt like just another name in his little black book.

"God, I'm such an idiot," I hissed.

When I heard the front door open, I turned off the head-lights of my car. I needed to get inside before my parents started asking questions, and I needed a fucking shower. I grabbed my purse and headed inside, ignoring the blatant smell of stale beer in the air.

"How was your first day, honey?" Mom asked.

I made my way up the stairs. "It was good. Long. I'm beyond exhausted."

Dad harrumphed. "He better not keep you late anymore. Your mother slaved over dinner."

I sniffed the air. "Yeah, takes a lot of work to order out pizza."

Dad yelled up at me, "Hey! You get back down here!"

I rolled my eyes. "Need a shower. Got another long day ahead of me tomorrow."

"Bella, I told you to get down here!"

I whipped around and pinned my father with an angry gaze. "Unless you want me down there to apologize for embarrassing me and almost costing me my job today, you can stuff it. The reason why I had to stay late in the first place was to try to show my new boss that I am dedicated to this job and that your drunken antics won't affect my workplace productivity. So, you want me home on time? Quit being a drunk."

Then, I stormed upstairs and locked myself in my bathroom before the tears started barreling down my cheeks.

❧ 10 ❧

Wyatt

I nodded as I walked through the front doors. "Miss Bella."

She didn't look up from her computer. "Mr. Remington."

I paused at her desk. "I take it you've had a good morning thus far?"

She still didn't look at me. "Of course. I hope you have, as well."

It was the same shit but a different morning. For days now, Bella and I had been tiptoeing around one another. And while her father hadn't come storming back in liquored up with vodka or beer, I'd been finding excuses to stop by her desk. Bidding her good morning was a prime opportunity to gauge her mood and determine if she could even look at me after what had happened a few days prior.

But, she never did.

Nevertheless, I kept pursuing it. I wanted her to look at me. I wanted to see whatever it was she felt she was hiding like a professional. So, I took improperly completed paperwork straight to her desk of my own volition. I had her come up to my office a few times to pick up things I ordered for her that kept coming in.

Like her name plaque for her desk.

Or her company credit card for making conference purchases.

Or the keys to her company car.

"You gave her a car?" Will asked.

I drew in a deep breath as the man stormed through my office door. "Yes, come in. Please, have a seat."

He placed his hands against my desk. "Since when do we shell out the money to give secretaries company cars, Wyatt?"

My fingers kept clacking against the keyboard. "Have you seen my email, by any chance? I haven't gotten responses back yet."

"Focus, Wyatt. We're talking about things that financially impact the company."

My eyes finally met his. "So am I."

He sighed. "Why in the world did you requisition a car for that girl?"

"Doesn't every department-head have one?"

He blinked. "Since when is a secretary the department-head of anything?"

I shrugged. "Since we hired Bella to be the presenting face of this company and gave her the ability to coordinate every other secretary's schedules for every individual department."

"Wyatt, we don't have a 'secretaries' department. They are simply aids to the *actual* departments we have."

I stood slowly to my feet. "So, what you're saying is that without those aids, our departments wouldn't run as smoothly."

He shook his head. "Oh, no. I see where this argument is going."

I slid my hands into my pockets. "Then, I'll save you the argument. Bella's getting this car. She's the face of this headquarters. She's the only secretary employed full-time with benefits. She's the sole coordinator of things like our conferences and out-of-town business ventures. She's getting the damn car."

Will straightened his back. "If she wrecks that car—"

I cut him off. "Our insurance will deal with it, just like it always does."

And when he didn't respond, I showed him out the same way he had come barging in.

However, I found myself distracted for the rest of the day. Even though everything had come in for Bella, I still wanted to see her. I still wanted to be around her. I just didn't have an appropriate excuse. That little spat with Will cost me my lunch hour, and I was thirty minutes behind on paperwork I had to have logged by the end of the day.

Still, I decided that I needed to make sure our prime secretary had eaten.

I made my way down to the main floor and silenced my footsteps. I heard Bella talking on the phone, but her voice was hushed. I furrowed my brow as I approached her desk from behind, trying to keep myself as quiet as possible. And when she turned toward her computer, I saw she had her cell phone propped against her shoulder.

"Daddy, I'm at work," she whispered, "can't this wait?"

I paused, holding my breath as Bella continued to speak.

"I can order you something. But—yes, Daddy, I know. I mean, that's great that Mom's—yes, there's sandwich meat—will you let me finish a sentence, please?"

My heart broke for her. She led a rough life, it seemed, and part of that was due to her father as well as my own. I wondered if she knew. I wondered if she had put it together yet. Had her father told her? Surely, she knew by now.

Maybe that's why she won't look at me anymore.

Bella sighed. "Daddy, I have to go. I'm already behind on work. And if Mom wants to get a job, that's completely her call. No one can babysit you while you drink yourself to death; that's your choice. Oh? Well, then whose choice is it, Dad, if not yours?"

I braced for it. I braced for the moment Bella's father told her everything and she stormed out of this place, never to return. But instead, she simply shook her head and hung up the phone. I saw her screen instantly light up before she pressed a button on the side. And when the screen lit up again, she shoved it into her purse.

So, I came around to the side of her desk. "Did you clock out for lunch?"

Bella almost leaped out of her chair. "Holy shi— I mean, uh... Mr. Remington. Hello. I didn't hear you, my apologies."

I leaned against her desk. "Didn't mean to frighten you."

Her eyes met mine for the first time since Monday. "Um, but yes. I—I did clock out for lunch. Why? Was I gone too long?"

I shook my head. "Just wanted to make sure you take your lunch hour. The company can be audited and fined if we don't adhere to the strict hiring practices laid out for us."

She nodded. "Well, I took a fifty-six-minute break and ate right there in the kitchen."

I drew in a deep breath through my nose. "Have you given the car a test drive yet?" I could've sworn she smiled softly at me.

"To be honest, I was thinking about doing that during my lunch break. But, I decided against it."

I grinned. "Why's that?"

I watched her go to respond before something stopped her. And all at once, her face shut down. Gone was the shadow of a smile, and gone was the playfulness in her voice. She quickly sat back down at her desk and turned to face her computer, typing away as if we hadn't just started a conversation.

"I'll let you know how it drives Monday once I come in," Bella said coolly.

I decided to call it like it was. "Bella, just because things happened between your father and mine doesn't mean things have to be this tense at work. I hope you know that."

She slowly turned around and looked up at me. "Between our fathers?"

I nodded. "Yeah, their feud and how it's affected them doesn't have to affect us."

She blinked. "What the hell are you talking about?"

Oh, no. "What?"

She stood to her feet. "What are you talking about right now, Wyatt?"

I shook my head. "Nothing to be discussed here."

She moved toward me like lightning, and in a flash, she was in my face. "Whatever it is you know about my father, you better spit it out now."

I took a step back. "I'm not having this conversation at work, Miss Bella."

She glared at me. "Then keep your mouth shut, Mr. Remington."

I decided to overlook her tone of voice. "However, if you'd like to discuss it—since your father hasn't with you, it seems —we can go get a coffee after work."

She narrowed her eyes. "Do you ever ask people for their time, Mr. Remington? Or do you simply demand it and expect people to follow through?"

Her words stopped me in my tracks. No one had ever

talked to me like this, let alone called me out. At least, not an employee, or any woman I had ever had relations with. I saw the anger in her eyes. I felt her frustration radiating out at me. And if I had a chance to get coffee with her, even if it was a bitter encounter, I figured it was better than what we'd been doing all week.

So, I sucked down my pride and clicked my tongue. "You have a point."

Her face softened. "I do? I mean, yeah. Of course, I do."

I chuckled softly. "Bella?"

Her eye twitched. "Yes, Wyatt?"

"Would you like to go get coffee after work with me and talk about this?"

And after she wiped the utter shock off her face, she said the words I had wanted to hear all along. "See you at five."

11

Bella

How I ended up driving my company vehicle to get coffee with Wyatt in the passenger's seat, I'd never know. Well, I had an inkling of an idea, but it was still a bad position to be in. Wyatt's cologne kept distracting me from the road. I was trying to prove to my boss that I'd be a good driver while trying not to pay attention to the fact that the damn car matched his outfit.

All black, from front to back.

The buttery-leather cradled me like a cloud. The cooling seats kept me calm in the harsh summer heat as we drove to my favorite coffee place. And Wyatt's figure sitting next to me dressed in black from head to toe had me aching for him in ways I hated to admit to. The man cut well in a suit, but dammit, black was his color. It brought out the sun-kissed nature of his skin as well as enhanced the brooding stare that he kept tossing my way every time I came to a stop.

As if he were trying to take a sneak peek into my soul.

"Bingo," I whispered.

Wyatt nodded. "Coolie's. This is a good place. I came here a lot back before I lived in town."

I eased into the parking lot. "This was my escape during school. I'd come here and study, and the baristas would always look the other way when I filled my coffee up one more time than was allowed."

He chuckled. "Sounds like a nice memory."

I parked the car. "Come on in. There's a coffee you have to try if they still serve it. It's not on the menu. One of those 'hidden items' sort of things. But it's fantastic."

He grinned at me. "Lead the way then, *Miss* Bella."

A shiver worked its way down my spine as I quickly scampered out of the car. I wasn't sure why Wyatt put that kind of emphasis on my name, and I didn't want to be in close quarters with him long enough to find out. I'd gotten myself into enough confusing trouble with him, and the last thing I needed was more of that. Nevertheless, I couldn't help but register the small things he did for me that seemed almost second-nature to him.

Like, opening the coffee shop door for me.

Or escorting me to the cashier with his hand against the small of my back.

Or him not even blinking an eye when he went to pay for my coffee and pastry.

Or him pulling out my chair for me to sit at a table in the corner I picked out for us.

Why did I put us in the corner again?

I didn't even know anymore.

"You know I could've paid. That would've been all right," I said.

He waved his hand in the air before sitting. "It's not an issue; don't worry about it."

"I also don't like it when people are flippant with things I say, even if what comes after can be construed as 'romantic.'"

His eyes held mine. "Are you always so harsh on your bosses?"

"I don't know, are you my boss right now? Or a friend?"

He leaned back. "Good question."

I mocked his movements. "So?"

He sipped his drink. "So."

I sighed. "Am I going to have to pull this story about our fathers out of you? Or, are you going to give it up willfully?"

He grinned. "I think I might enjoy watching you pull something out of me."

I blinked. "All right, I'm heading out."

He leaned forward. "Wait, wait, wait. Will you just take a breath, please?"

My eyes danced across his face. "How did that 'please' taste?"

He grimaced. "Like lemon in rotting milk."

I barked with laughter. "All right, I'll bite. What is it you know about my father that I don't?"

"I'm honestly shocked he hasn't told you already."

"Told me what?"

He sipped his coffee. "The rodeo accident?"

I furrowed my brow. "You mean, the one my father was in?"

He nodded. "The one both of our fathers were in."

I paused. "I'm not following."

He licked his lips. "Our dads competed regularly against one another. Did you know that?"

"Honestly? I wasn't one for the rodeos. I mean, I went because Mom took me. But, once I was old enough to start staying home by myself, I usually opted not to go."

He nodded. "Well, they were heavy competitors. Your father and mine were always vying for the top spot in the state for steer wrestling."

"I'm familiar with what my father did, yes."

He sighed. "During one of their competitions, they were head to head. Both of them had identical scores in every single way, and it was the first time that had ever happened. So, the county commission decided to hold a steer wrestling competition with just the two of them. And whoever roped the steer and got it down first took the top spot."

"Sounds fair enough."

"Until my father's horse crashed into your father's, yes."

I blinked. "Wait. What?"

"That's what happened. My father's horse crashed into your

father's horse, and it knocked them both to the ground. The steer ran out of control, stomped onto your father's back before the handlers could get to him, and that's how your father got injured."

I felt my vision tunneling. "That's not what happened."

Wyatt narrowed his eyes. "Bella, are you okay?"

I scooted my chair back. "That—that isn't what happened."

He reached his hand out for me. "Just come back to the table. You look a little pale, take a sip of—"

I leaped to my feet. "Stop telling me what to do, you pompous windbag!"

The entire coffee shop came to a standstill, and I felt all eyes on me. My face flushed with anger and my fists clenched at my sides as the world seemed to be spinning all around me. I felt dizzy. I felt weak. I felt belittled and idiotic. But what was worse was that I felt lied to.

I just didn't know who was lying to me.

"Bella, look at me." Wyatt placed his hands on my shoulders, and my watery eyes slid up his body. "Will you sit for me? Please?" he asked.

I let him guide me back into my chair before the hustle and bustle of the coffee shop struck up. But the damage had already been done. People would be talking about my outburst in this damn place for the next week.

"Wyatt, that isn't—"

He scooted his chair to sit beside me. "What do you think happened?"

I slowly looked over at him as a tear trickled down my cheek. "I saw my father get into that accident. They were riding around on horses and shooting T-shirts into the stands. Dad got bucked off his horse, and it landed on him. I was there. I saw it with my own two eyes."

He took my hand in his. "Are you sure that's what you saw? Or, are you remembering something you were told as a perceived memory?"

I didn't know what to believe. "I have to go."

"Bella, you need to—"

I pulled away from him. "You really need to get that demanding thing under control. It's going to ruin you."

He caught my arm as I tried to walk away. "My father didn't know that yours had been injured."

I closed my eyes. "I can't do this right now. I need to get home."

He spun me around. "My father went down on his horse, too. He didn't even realize something was wrong until he got back up on his horse and saw the handlers fielding the steer. And by the time he went to go see what was going on with your father, a rodeo hand had the reins and was pulling his horse—with him on top—out of the ring."

As much as I didn't want to, I forced myself to look into Wyatt's eyes. With tears marring my skin and dripping down my neck, I gazed into the eyes of a man who had no reason to lie to me. I studied his intense gaze, the worry rushing behind his eyes. I felt his grip on my arm, and it pulled me from whatever trance had a hold on me, and I drew in a deep breath.

"You're not lying to me, are you?" I asked softly.

His hand fell away from my arm. "What reason do I have to lie about something like this?"

My exact point.

I slowly sat down in my chair and grabbed my coffee. I chugged it back, forcing the burn to pull me out of my hazy, angry trance. Now, I understood, and it made so much fucking sense. I mean, my father's response to my working at the Remington's company had me so perplexed, until now.

But, where in the world had my memory come from?

Was my father injured twice?

"Bella?"

My tired gaze found his stare. "Yes?"

"Are you going to be okay to drive home?"

I scoffed. "During a moment like this, you're worried about me scuffing up the company car?"

He shook his head. "No. I'm worried about you scuffing up yourself."

I sank against my chair. "I'm sorry. I just—"

He licked his lips. "It's a lot to take in at once, I know. Especially since it seems like..." He didn't finish the sentence, but I knew what he was about to say.

Especially since it seems like I've been lied to.

I sat there in silence, polishing off my coffee and picking at my pastry. And the entire time I sat there, so did Wyatt. He didn't have to, but he did. I didn't know why he waited, but I was thankful for it. I didn't want to be alone right now, and maybe he sensed that. But, for whatever reason, I was glad to have him there because the silence wasn't at all awkward.

In fact, it was pleasantly comfortable, and as he sat beside me, I felt his leg rest against my thigh. His arm connected with my shoulder as if moving to be a prop for my tired body. And I leaned against him with all the thankfulness in the world as I rested myself against him while soaking up his comforting warmth.

If he was honest with me, I need to be honest with him.

My entire body stiffened, and I knew he felt it.

"Bella?"

I sat up. "Sorry. Just—lost myself in thought for a second."

He turned to face me. "Want to talk about it?"

I shook my head but couldn't look at him. "Nah, I'm good."

"Bella."

"Wyatt."

"What's on your mind?"

I shook my head. "It's really nothing."

He snickered. "Doesn't look like nothing."

I rolled my eyes. "I think one big topic is enough for today."

"So, there's another big topic to be discussed?"

I groaned. "Please, Wyatt, just leave it."

"Why do I get the feeling I should do the exact opposite, then?"

"Because you're stubborn?"

He stared a hole into the profile of my face. "I think if we're here to talk and throw things out on the table that we didn't know about previously, it's only fair that you don't keep me hanging on this ledge alone. Because whatever you have to say, it can't be as bad as what I just told you."

I scoffed. "Really?"

He nodded. "Really."

I finally turned to face him. "Is that what you think?"

"That's what I know," he said before he took a sip of his coffee.

Better now than never. "Fine. You asked for it; just remember that."

He swallowed. "I'm listening."

So, I drew in a quick breath. "Up until the other night, I was technically a virgin."

And when his jaw unhinged in shock, his hand went limp, spilling the rest of his coffee into his lap.

12

Wyatt

A *virgin?*

Did I hear her right?

"Shit," I hissed.

My coffee hit my lap, and it felt like my dick was on fire. I shot up from my seat as the cup tumbled from my hand, and Bella stood along with me. I heard her say something about napkins before she dashed off, but all I could do was slowly raise my eyes as I watched her pull those cheap paper things out of the canister by the coffee station.

Now, things made so much sense.

Like the little bit of blood left behind in my truck after our encounter. I had just thought Bella had started her period, and that was why she rushed off as quickly as she had. Or the way she couldn't quite look me in the face this week. But now, I understood. Now, it all made sense.

I saw her through a completely different lens, and I chastised myself silently for being an absolute fuckwad.

"Here, let me help," Bella said breathlessly.

I grabbed her wrist as she went to dab at my crotch, and I glared down at her. "I got it. You sit."

She swallowed hard. "Oh—okay. Here."

I took the napkins from her hand and focused on cleaning myself off. Thank fuck, I decided to wear an all-black suit today. I drew in a sobering breath as I eased myself back down, feeling Bella's eyes on me the entire time. I cleaned off the seat before I tossed the napkins down onto the table, and before I blinked enough to focus my gaze, one of the baristas had another coffee set in front of me that I didn't bother touching.

"Thanks," I said mindlessly.

If the barista said something, I didn't hear it. I was too busy staring at Bella. I was waiting for her to say, "just kidding!" I was waiting for her to tell me it was nothing but a joke made at my expense. However, all she did was look at me through those beautiful doe eyes of hers, and guilt pooled in my chest. Had I known she was a virgin, I would've done things so much differently. And I wasn't sure if that made me a better man or a shittier one.

"Wyatt?" she asked softly.

Anyone's first time should be better than that. "I want to start by apologiz—"

"Where the hell is my daughter?"

The second I heard Bella's father's voice boom through the coffee shop, I peered over my shoulder. Bella shot to her feet as her jaw hit the floor and I saw her father barge through those front doors. I couldn't tell by his voice that he was drunk, but his footsteps said otherwise. He kept veering left and right, trying to walk in a straight line as he held his finger up toward his daughter's face.

"No daughter of mine's gonna date someone like this man!" he exclaimed.

And when he hiccupped, tears crested Bella's eyes. "Daddy, keep your voice down. We're just—"

He tripped over his own two feet, and I jumped out of my chair to catch him. But, he shoved me away as if I held the plague on the tip of my fingers. His eyes shot crooked daggers in my direction before he shoved himself between me and his daughter, his back to me as he stared down at Bella.

I didn't like this one damn bit.

"You will never date a Remington. All those boys are off-limits to you. Got it?" her father growled.

Bella took his hand. "Just take a breath, Dad. We were just getting coffee. This isn't a—"

"The hell it isn't!" he yelled as he peered over his shoulder at me. "I know exactly what you're doing, and it isn't going to work. My daughter is good, and I won't have you ruining that for her."

I cocked my head. "I have no idea what you mean."

He whipped around to face me. "Yes, you do, you slimy little snake."

Bella gasped. "Dad!"

He turned back around, almost stumbling off his feet again so badly that I had to catch him. Only this time, he didn't have the energy to shove me away as I held him steady while the coffee shop watched in horror.

"I know what men like him are like. I know what his entire *family* is like! And I will not have my daughter flaunting herself around with some boytoy who isn't nearly good enough for her. You got that?"

I leaned down to her father's ear. "I really think we should take this outside, Mr. Lancaster. Someone might call the police, and I'd hate for you to get arrested because you're making another stupid mistake."

He growled. "The only stupid mistake I've made is allowing my daughter to take this job in the first place."

Bella barked with laughter. "Dad, you didn't allow me to do anything in the first place. I am my own person, and I make my own decisions, just like you choose every single day to drown your sorrows in beer instead of getting the help you need."

I finally pulled my arms away from her father. "She's right. She's her own woman and—"

"Fuck off, or I'll make you fuck off." He didn't even bother looking at me as he insulted me.

I wasn't sure what popped inside of me, but the second I blinked, I was between Bella and her father. Her hand pressed against my back, trembling in fright and worry as I stood toe to toe with Mr. Lancaster. I cleared the top of his head by a good five inches, and the way he had to crane his head back to keep my eyes in view was entertaining to me.

I loved it when a man thought he could step to my rhythm. But, I hated it when a man thought he could control a woman's actions simply because he believed he owned her.

"I'm not sure what you came here to do today, Mr. Lancaster, but allow me to correct a few things. One, your daughter and I are not out on a date. If we were, I'd be driving, we'd be having dinner, she'd be dressed up, and I'd be treating her to a full-scale night out on the town. Secondly, the mere fact that you feel you have to get drunk before you come in here and attempt to bark at your daughter tells me that you don't have the kind of guts you think you do. You just don't like the fact that Bella doesn't hate my family the way you hate my family. And third of all—and listen up, because this is the important one—you will never, ever address Bella the way you just did in my presence. Because if it happens again? I'll be the one calling the police and having you arrested. Understood?"

Her father's eye twitched. "You really want to do this now, boy?"

I narrowed my eyes. "Whether or not you want to believe it, your rodeo accident wasn't my father's fault. Accidents happen all the time, and that one moment didn't just change your life; it changed my father's as well. Not once did he ever sign up for another rodeo after that. Not once did he ever compete after that. You were *both* changed, and to hold your daughter to some superimposed, selfish vendetta you have against our family—"

"That's enough!" Bella's voice ricocheted off the corners of the coffee shop and stopped me in my tracks.

I swallowed down the rest of my words as her father peered around my body, and for once, I actually saw worry for his daughter in his eyes. I turned and found Bella's glare filled with tears. Her fists were clenched at her sides, and her back was straight and determined.

And her eyes locked on me.

"That's enough," she hissed.

I swallowed down the rest of my anger. "Bella, you have my sincerest—"

She held her hand up, stopping my words in my tracks. And without another word, she moved around me to get to her father. She linked her arm around his and shot me one last glance before murmuring something to him I didn't catch.

Then, I watched the two of them walk gingerly toward the coffee shop doors.

Standing there, all alone in that shop, was one of the lower points of my life. What I thought was coming to Bella's defense had been actions that pushed her farther away, and I hated that. I didn't want this distance between us. I didn't want us to keep tiptoeing around one another. But, how in the fuck was I supposed to fix this.

"It's okay, Dad. Get it up," Bella said softly.

I heard her voice fluttering through the open doors as a

barista raced out to help them. I watched her father bend over and throw up on the concrete near the company car while Bella rubbed his back. Another barista rushed out there with a pail of water while the original one who had raced out there tried to wipe his face off and get some water into his system. And when Bella peered back through the windows at me, her eyes hardened.

I watched as they cleaned up her father. I watched as they climbed into Bella's company car. Then, I watched as they left. With all eyes on me and the coffee shop completely silent, I relegated myself to a walk back to my office. I needed the fresh air to clear my head. I needed the time to parse through what the fuck had just happened. So, I picked up my coffee, meandered my way through the tables and chairs, and set my sights on HQ, even though it was six damn miles away.

13

Bella

I sighed as I sat in the driveway of my house. I say "house" because it didn't feel like home anymore. As my father snored in the backseat with vomit still crusted to his teeth, I stared at the garage door as it slowly opened. It inched itself up, panel by panel until my mother's tired and disheveled figure emerged from the darkness.

You deserve better than this, Mom.

I rolled down my window. "Hey, there."

She bent forward. "I tried to get him to stay here. I even took the keys to the truck. But, he must've called someone."

I sighed. "Probably an Uber. I put the app on his phone a few weeks back in an attempt to combat his drunk driving."

She peeked in back. "You want to leave him here to sleep it off?"

I shrugged. "Not particularly. This is my company car. I'd like it to not smell like puke."

She nodded slowly. "Then, help me get him inside."

It took all of the strength my mother and I had to hoist his ass out of the backseat and into the house. And even then, the only thing we could do was flop him down into a recliner and cover him with a blanket. The man snored away as if we hadn't done a thing, and when the smell of dinner pulled me into the kitchen, I saw Mom brushing away tears from her cheeks.

So, I started massaging her shoulders.

"I'm so sorry he's always like this. You deserve so much better, Bella."

I kissed the back of her head. "So do you, Mom."

She shook her head. "Why can't he snap out of it? Why can't he see what he's been doing to us all this time?"

I shrugged. "I don't know. I really don't."

Silence fell between us as I helped her finish up the rest of dinner. But, as we sat down to eat the soup and fresh bread she baked for all of us, I couldn't stop myself.

"What really happened at that rodeo all those years ago?" I asked.

Mom froze, her spoon halfway to her mouth as her eyes gravitated to me. "What?"

I set my bread down. "The rodeo, Mom. Someone in this family needs to start talking about it."

"Well, that's your father's thing to talk about. Not mine."

"So, was Wyatt right? Because he told me that no one ran into Dad or anything like that. He said it was a simple steer wrestling competition to settle a tied score, and Dad just fell and got trampled by the steer."

Mom's stare held my gaze. "Is that what you think happened?"

I shrugged. "Judging by what you and Dad told me, apparently what I thought happened isn't actually what happened at all. And if I'm going to be working for the Remington family, don't you think I have a right to know what took place?"

Her eyes fell to her soup. "Again, not my story to tell."

"Mom, this is serious. This is getting to be too much. Dad is on my tail every second of every day now because I work for Wyatt and his brothers, and it's not going to change until—"

His tired voice sounded from behind us. "Until you know what's really going on."

Mom gasped as I looked over and found my father leaning heavily against the doorway. I knew he was still drunk, but he seemed a bit more coherent after throwing up the contents of his stomach outside of the coffee shop. He stumbled to the bread and tore off a chunk of it before chewing it down as quickly as he could. Then, he reached the fridge and pulled out a bottle of water before coming and sitting down at the head of the table.

"You sure you're ready for the story as to what happened?" Dad asked.

I nodded. "I've been ready for a while. I need the truth, for many reasons."

He leaned back. "You're not gonna like it."

I set my spoon down. "Try me."

He tore off another chunk of bread. "Remington, Sr.'s horse tripped mine up."

I blinked. "Wait, really?"

"Really, really. Saw it out of the corner of my eye. I was comin' up on that steer, and he didn't like it, and I saw him bring his horse closer to mine. I saw their hooves collide. I felt the jolt of his horse's body against my own. He broke the damn rules, and not once did they call him out for it. They just let me plummet to the ground before my horse ran off."

"Did anyone rush to help you?"

He shrugged. "They should have. Hell, Senior should've gotten off that fucking horse himself and helped after what he caused. But, he kept riding. He kept chasing that damned steer around before it turned and headed straight for me. And instead of cutting the damned thing off, Senior let that fucking animal stomp right over me. Took all four hooves to the back that day, and that man didn't give enough fucks to get off his damn horse and come see about me."

I shook my head slowly. "Why don't I remember this?"

Mom patted my forearm. "It happened during a sleepover you were having with a bunch of your friends. You were clear across town all weekend when it happened."

I swallowed hard. "But, I remember that T-shirt incident so clearly."

Mom sighed. "And that's my fault. I just—as you grew up, it became harder and harder to rehash what had happened. It was so traumatic for both your father and me that one day when you asked us what happened because you couldn't remember, the T-shirt story just came blurting out. I figured it was easier on all of us to rehash *that* moment instead of, well, you know."

My eyes panned back over to Dad. "And you were okay with this? With just—lying to me like that?"

Dad shrugged. "Saved you from the truth. Kept your innocence a bit more. You were young, and you didn't need to be burdened with shit like that."

I drew in a sobering breath. "Wyatt told me his father didn't know you were injured until after he roped the steer."

The table fell silent before Dad's stare turned hot. "They already sinking their lying little teeth into you?"

I scoffed. "That's rich coming from you right now, considering what we just got done talking about. Because of you two, I've been walking around with a lie I didn't know was a lie all of my life. So, you don't have a high road to take with this conversation."

Mom hissed, "Shut up, both of you. We're eating dinner, and this should be an orderly and kind affair. Got it?"

But, Dad didn't stop glaring at me. Even as he stood to his feet, his eyes never left my face. Even as he walked over to my side, his eyes danced along my features.

Until those dreaded words fell from his lips. "You fucked him, didn't you?"

Mom gasped. "Colton! What in the world?"

He held his finger up to Mom. "Can it, Charlotte. I'm talking to our daughter."

I stood to my feet. "Where do you get off asking me such a question?"

Mom tugged on Dad's wrist. "Colton, sit down. You're creating chaos out of nothing. All she wants is answers, and since she's the sole provider of this family right now, she deserves them."

Dad pulled away from her grip. "Did you screw around with that boy? Huh? Did you let him defile you?"

I took a step back. "I don't even know who you are anymore."

Dad clenched his fists. "Answer me, dammit!"

I didn't answer him, though. All I did was turn on my heels and race for the front door. I heard Dad stumbling after me while Mom yelled at him, but my sober feet would always be quicker than his drunken boots. They argued and shouted at one another as I raced back out to my car. With my purse clutched tightly in my hand, I unlocked the door and cranked the engine with the touch of a button. I leaped in just as Dad made his way for the front door, and as I threw the car into reverse without so much as buckling my seatbelt, I saw his crooked form standing on the porch.

"No daughter of mine will be a slut for those boys!" he roared.

Tears slid down my cheeks effortlessly as I blazed a trail out of the neighborhood. I set my sights on the main road out of town, wanting nothing more than to get away from everyone and everything as my heart broke. My soul was drowning. I was lost and alone and tied to a place in this world I didn't even want. I sobbed with joy as the town fell behind me. I sighed with relief as the sign ushering me out of Conroe greeted me with its white and green façade.

I decided to ride off into the darkness, with no plan and no destination in mind.

Hopefully, to find a piece of solace all to myself.

What a hell of a first week at work.

I white-knuckled the steering wheel as abandoned farmland greeted me on both sides of the two-lane road. And the longer I drove, the more I contemplated quitting. I mean, there was no coming back from all of this, right? My father would only make my life more miserable until Wyatt did nothing but resent me. And besides, no job was worth this heartache. No job was worth dredging up a years-long feud I didn't even fucking know about until Dad stumbled into my work drunk as a skunk.

Yet, the idea of quitting hurt my soul.

Sobs jumped forth, hiccupping my chest. My hands started getting shaky, which caused the car to become uneasy on the road. So, instead of continuing to drive and put my life in danger, I pulled into the first meadow of wildflowers I came upon. Much of the abandoned farmland in and around Conroe had become overgrown with wild trees and weeds.

But, a few of the pastures that had once held thriving animals wafted in the summer breeze with all the colors of the rainbow.

So, I pulled into the middle of the wildflower meadow, leaned my seat back, and opened up the sunroof above me before I let the tears I'd been holding back all my life freely fall with no one around to judge me in the process.

14

Wyatt

I tapped my pen against the desk as I stared at my computer screen. From the corner of my eye, the untouched stack of folders I still had to whittle away at taunted me like an old memory. With Ryan gone, there was more work than ever, and I usually welcomed that kind of distraction.

But this evening, something else entirely held me hostage.

Just do it. That's why the cars have them.

Something in my gut didn't feel right. Something hadn't sat well with me ever since I'd gotten back to my office. And as the clock on my computer ticked over to nine in the evening, I still couldn't shake the feeling that something was wrong.

Very, very wrong.

With Bella.

"Just one peek," I murmured.

I placed my pen down against my desk and started typing away at my keyboard. All of our company cars came equipped with GPS locators for various reasons. It helped with emergencies or if our employees got into an accident and we needed to be able to locate them. It also helped us in other emergent situations, like one of our employee's cars being stolen a couple of years back. And while I didn't want to invade Bella's personal life, I wanted to make sure she had gotten home safely. And pulling up the GPS locator data might give me some solace.

"Come on," I murmured.

It took longer than I wished for the data to populate. But, once it did, panic gripped my throat. Bella's car wasn't anywhere near her house. In fact, it wasn't anywhere near the city limits of Conroe. I picked the pen back up and jotted down the GPS coordinates before tearing away from my desk. I scooped up my things and locked up for the evening, convinced that something terrible had happened to her after our rousing conversation at the coffee shop.

So, I locked up shop, dashed down to my car, and plugged in the coordinates.

Why the fuck is she out in the middle of nowhere?

For the first time in my life, I was terrified. Bella had no business being out there, especially with the company car. What if she had stalled out trying to get somewhere? What if her car had been stolen from her home? What if she was hurt and had to abandon her car for some reason? So many devastating ideas rushed through my mind as I blazed a trail out of town.

"Maybe she's just at that restaurant," I whispered to myself.

The second I flew past the goodbye sign as people exited Conroe, I turned my sights to the side of the road. She was somewhere on my left, and all I had to do was keep an eye out for a blacked-out, supped-up car in the middle of nowhere. But, part of me wondered if she had been venturing out to that restaurant where we first went out for dinner. This was the same road we had driven. This was the only pathway to get up that massive hill before even partaking in the restaurant's views.

The idea of her going somewhere I had introduced her to made my heart soar. But, when I finally came across her car in a field of wildflowers, my heart sank.

I turned off my truck lights and eased off the road. I didn't know if the car was abandoned or if she was in it, and if she was out here, I didn't want to startle her. I inched along, feeling my tires crushing flowers beneath its treads as I pulled up beside the car with its tinted windows.

And when I cut the engine to my vehicle, I heard her soft sobs wafting from the sunroof she had open. "Oh, Bella," I whispered.

I slid out of my truck and softly padded around to the driver's side. A soft breeze kicked up, ruffling my hair and fluttering my suit jacket as I slid my left hand into my pocket. With my right hand, I knocked softly with my knuckles against the tinted glass.

Then, I watched the window roll down before I saw Bella wiping at her tears.

"What in the world are you doing out here?" she asked breathlessly.

I pulled my cell phone out of my pocket. "All company cars have a GPS equipped in case they get stolen."

She sighed. "Wonderful."

I slid my phone back into my pocket. "Mind if I join you?"

She scoffed. "Do I have a choice?"

I nodded. "With me, you do."

Her eyes met mine, and I saw something wafting behind them. "Yeah, sure. Door's unlocked."

I walked around and dipped down into the leather seat next to her with nothing but the center console separating us. I closed the door and locked us inside, just to give us more of a semblance of privacy. If Bella heard the locks click, she didn't act as if she did.

"Do you want to talk about it?" I asked.

She softly shook her head but didn't say anything.

"Do you want me to guess why you're out here?"

She shook her head again but still didn't say anything.

"Do you want me to shut up so you can think straight?"

She snickered but still shook her head. However, I saw her wringing her hands in her lap. And instinctively, almost as if my body moved before my brain had the idea, I cupped my left hand over both of hers nestled in her lap.

"I'm right here," I said softly. And those three words were enough to unleash the waterfall.

She hung her head as if she were ashamed of something and sobbed. I swear to fuck on high, I'd never seen nor heard anyone cry like this in all my life, especially a woman. The heart-wrenching sound broke my heart. It was almost like the aural equivalent of death itself. I heard Bella's spirit dying upon the sobs that fell from her lips. I felt her body giving up as she slowly sank toward the steering wheel. Her hands trembled against my palm as her tears streaked her cheek, then her neck, then her chest. And as I blinked back my own tears of sorrow, I drew in a broken breath through my nose.

"What can I do to make you smile?"

As if her actions answered my question, her body fell toward me. I released her hands and wrapped my arms around her, guiding her cheek to my shoulder. She leaned over the center console, tucking her wet face against the crook of my neck. So, I rubbed my hand up and down her arm as she sought out whatever shred of comfort I could afford her.

"It's going to be all right. I promise," I whispered. I kissed the top of Bella's head without thinking about it, and her sobs started to taper off. I closed my eyes, listening to the breezy wind as it rushed against the open sunroof above our heads. The car felt cramped, especially with this damn console between us, which led me to a proposition that seemed more asinine than most.

"Come. We're going to go lay in the bed of my truck."

Bella snickered. "Yeah, because that worked well for us last time."

I chuckled. "The view of the stars will be better there, and I'll be able to comfort you properly."

She picked her head up. "Don't I know it."

My lips downturned into a frown. "I'm more than that kind of man, Bella."

Her eyes flickered over to me. "I know. At least, I'd like to believe as such."

No, really. I'm better than that. "Seriously, come on. I've got blankets and pillows and everything to make this more comfortable. Plus, we'll be able to smell the flowers."

"Remember what I told you about demanding someone's time?"

I chewed on the inside of my cheek. "Will you please join me for a night of stargazing and comforting in the bed of my truck?"

She slowly turned her red, puffy eyes toward me. "Yeah, sure. I don't have anything else to lose."

Her words made my eye twitch. Dammit, this beautiful woman deserved better than what she was getting. And yet, I didn't know how to salvage the situation. Still, when she got out of her car, I quickly followed suit and took the liberty of setting things up. As she meandered around the back of the car, I practically lunged into the bed of my truck. I pulled out blankets and pillows and all sorts of things to make the floorboard more comfortable for us to lay in. Then, with no sheer shield to cover us from the night sky, I held out my hand and helped Bella up onto the platform with me before we hunkered down against the blankets.

"Come here," I said softly.

She wiggled next to me and slid her leg over mine. I held out my arm, feeling her cheek press against my bicep before she wiggled herself a bit closer. Bella curled around me, tucking her face back against the crook of my neck. And as I let my fingertips travel all around the parts of her body I could find, she started crying again.

"It's going to be okay, I swear it," I whispered.

She sobbed so hard she started struggling to breathe.

"Sh-sh-sh-sh-sh. It's all right. It's just the two of us."

Her body violently shook with the force of her sobs. I had no idea how long she had held this all inside, but it all came pouring out, and it worried me. I heard her struggling to breathe. I felt her tears and her snot dripping against my skin. Against my suit. Against my body. Her muscles contracted and released as if they didn't know whether they were coming or going.

And in a desperate attempt to calm her down, I gripped her chin with my fingers. "Please, hearing you cry is killing me," I whispered.

I pulled her gaze to mine, and the utter sorrow etched into her features caused tears to spring to my own eyes.

Don't cry, Wyatt. Don't do it.

"I'm– I'm– I–I–I– I'm sor—sorry for—"

In a flash as quick as a lightning bug's ass going out, my

lips found hers. I captured those salted pillows against my own and allowed my tongue to push through the barrier. I held myself against her body, lapping softly at the roof of her mouth as her body froze against mine.

Then, with one last stroke of my tongue, she melted against me.

"It's okay," I said in between kisses, "I've got you. You're safe with me. Always."

The kisses were innocent at first. A desperate attempt to quell her soul that was crying out for solace. But, when her tongue fell against mine, I felt her legs part for me. Gone was her encompassing nature as she sought out my comfort, and instead, she opened her body to me for the taking. Her legs spread as she rolled onto her back. Her hands gripped the back of my suit coat as my hands planted onto either side of her head. Before I knew it, I found myself hovering over the most beautiful woman Conroe had ever etched from the DNA that ran through the town's veins.

And as I pulled back, my eyes dancing between hers, I found myself in the same position I had been in less than a week ago.

Only this time, I was determined to give her the experience she should have had the first time around.

15

Bella

I gazed up into Wyatt's eyes and saw my reflection. And I didn't like the look on my face. My cheeks were puffy, and my eyes were almost swollen shut with the force of my exhausted crying. My legs felt weak, and the longer I laid against the bed of his truck, the more tired I became. But, feeling his body sink against mine rejuvenated me in ways I'd never experienced before. Feeling his lips against my own filled me with a happiness I couldn't put words to.

And as his face came closer to mine, my legs spread effortlessly.

The second our lips collided again, my arms snaked around his neck. His hands traveled along my body, massaging my tits until my puckered peaks were aching for his tongue. I sucked on his lower lip, listening as he growled and rolled against me. And the thickness of his girth spurred me on.

In a flurry of wet kisses and nipped skin, our clothes were shed. I felt his muscles against my softness, etching their imprint against me forever. My pussy quivered for attention as he covered my body with kisses. His tongue lapped down my neck before he paused to nuzzle against my pulse point, sending me shooting to the heavens with every kiss of his heated lips as he traveled farther down my body.

Until he was perched between my legs.

"Oh, God," I said breathlessly.

He slid my legs over his shoulders. "Bella."

"Yeah?"

"Look at me, beautiful."

I raised up and found his starlit eyes gazing up at me. "What's up?"

He smiled softly. "Are you okay with this?"

Warmth trickled through my body. "I'm more than okay with it."

Without another word said, I watched his lips touch down against my pussy. For the first time in my life, I felt the heat of a man's mouth against my core, and it sent me spiraling into the darkness of the sky above me. The night blanketed us as his tongue breached my folds, unleashing the juices they had been holding back. And the growl he let loose against my swollen clit caused my back to arch.

"Holy shit," I groaned.

My hands flew into his hair. I pulled him closer as he

licked all the way up my trembling slit. My eyes rolled back, and my hips bucked against him as his hands tried to pin me to the floorboard of his truck bed. But, my wanton movements were too much for him to bear.

So, he got onto his knees, wrapped his arms around my hips, and pulled me upright until nothing but the middle of my back up to my head rested met the bed.

"Holy shit," I hissed.

I watched him lick up my slit again before diving deep between my folds. I felt suspended and helpless as pleasure washed its way through my veins. I dug my nails into the blankets beneath us. I locked my legs behind his head and squeezed my eyes shut. That same tightening sensation in my gut overwhelmed me, robbing me of my very breath as I choked out his name.

"Wy–att. Ple–ease. I need—"

With one last deep lick of his tongue, I fell over the edge. I shook against him as he sucked my clit between his lips, tickling the tip of it with his tongue. Electricity stood every hair on my body up on end. Joy clouded my mind as my heart sang out in glory.

And when my body collapsed against the weight of my orgasm, he settled me back down against the truck before tossing my legs over his shoulders again.

"Wyatt," I whispered.

His thick dick pressed against my entrance before he paused. "Are you all right?"

I nodded, but I couldn't open my eyes. "Please. I need to feel you again."

He entered me in one swift thrust that bulged my eyes out of my head. He folded me in half, pinning me beneath him before he captured my lips. His heated snaps against my pussy shook me to my core, causing my tits to bounce. I watched him bury his face in my cleavage. I felt his tongue licking at my nipples. I wrapped my hands around his wrists, clinging to him for dear life as ecstasy robbed me of my voice. And as my jaw unhinged in silent pleasure, I quickly fell over the edge again.

"Oh, that's it," he growled, "milk that dick, beautiful. Yes. Holy fuck, I'm gonna come. I'm gonna come, Bella. *Fuck*."

The second he exploded inside of me, my body collapsed in exhaustion. I laid there, with my knees against my chest, feeling the most amazing man I'd ever met fill me to the brim. Our intermingled juices poured from my entrance, making its way to my asshole. And as his balls quivered against my skin, my legs languidly slipped from his shoulders before Wyatt collapsed on top of me.

"I gotcha," I whispered against his ear. "Just rest."

Euphoria took hold of my existence as we laid there with his cock still sheathed in my warmth. I sighed with content, freed of the anger and the sadness that had washed over me in the middle of the meadow that night. Wyatt mustered just enough strength to search around for a blanket before pulling it over our naked bodies. And when he finally rolled off to the side, he pulled me along until my head rested against his chest.

"That feels good," I whispered.

"I'm glad," he murmured.

His fingertips slid up and down my spine as I looked out at the stars. Well, as we both looked up at the stars, really. They twinkled with happiness, almost as if they were cheering us on, and the thought made me smile. Wyatt kissed the top of my head, and I nuzzled against him. I felt his heart beating against my ear, creating a rhythmic sound that brought me more comfort than his embrace had.

Then, out of nowhere, I heard the words I was pretty certain no one had ever heard Wyatt Remington say in his entire life.

"I'm sorry, Bella."

I blinked. "For what?"

His fingers started running through my hair. "For... everything really. It's kind of an all-encompassing apology."

I turned my gaze up to look at him. "I still don't understand."

He shrugged. "I'm sorry for our fathers. How they're acting, and what happened between them. For what happened at the coffee shop and how I overstepped my boundaries."

I licked my lips. "Are you apologizing for what happened *to* us?" And when he didn't answer, I propped myself up. "Wyatt?"

He didn't look at me. "Yes?"

I slid up his body a bit. "Are you apologizing for what happened between us?"

He swallowed so hard I saw his Adam's apple bob two times in a row. "Part of me feels I should be."

"But you're not?"

He finally looked at me. "Is that bad?"

I smiled before I kissed his lips softly. "No. It's not bad. You couldn't have possibly known, and it wasn't as if I objected or anything."

He leaned up and kissed my lips a bit more fervently. "A first time for anyone should always be special, though. Not so random, like what you experienced."

I shrugged. "It was special to me, and it certainly wasn't random."

The shadow of a smile played against his lips. "You were eyeballing me, weren't you?"

I laid my head back down against his chest. "Hey, not my fault you rock a suit the way you do."

His chuckle reverberated throughout his body, and the soothing vibrations eased my eyes closed. I snuggled tightly against him, feeling his arm bring me even closer after I stopped moving. I tossed my leg between his, and I wrapped my arm around his waist. I cuddled close against his heart, allowing the beating of it to ease me into an effortless sort of trance. And I could've sworn I felt the earth around me leap for joy.

The wind rippled through the trees, causing branches to clap together. The wildflowers of the meadow swayed back and forth, fluttering their petals in joyful glee. It whistled around the corners of Wyatt's truck, singing us a small tune that only our ears could hear. And when I drew in my first deep, unbroken breath since parking in this field, I let my eyes fall closed.

"Bella?"

I hummed softly. "Hmmm?"

His hand stalled out in the middle of my back. "Have you ever taken a step back and wondered how different your life would be if you hadn't made the decisions you had?"

My brow ticked with confusion. "All the time. Why?"

He paused. "No reason."

I giggled softly before pressing a kiss against his chest. "Well, if you ever want to talk about the reason that will eventually rear its head, just know I'm here."

He kissed the top of my head. "I appreciate that. Thank you."

A chorus of crickets kicked up in the distance, and their chirping played in time with the wafts of wind caressing our naked bodies. I snuggled against Wyatt, feeling his muscles relaxing beneath me as darkness slowly pulled me under. I felt myself falling asleep, and yet I didn't give a shit about it.

Because as far as I was concerned, Wyatt's arms were the safest place I could have been, even though we were naked and vulnerable in the middle of a field.

16

Wyatt

I drew in a deep breath as I started packing up my things. Bella's second week of work went off without a hitch, and there had been no drama from her father in sight. So, I made my way downstairs in the hopes of convincing her to have coffee with me again. We hadn't talked much since our encounter in the meadow, and I didn't want that to become a regular thing for us. I didn't want us to keep hooking up and not talking about it.

She deserved better than that.

"Another successful week in the books," I said as I approached her desk.

Bella logged out of her computer. "I was just about to say the same thing when I heard your footsteps behind me."

I leaned against her desk. "And how did you know it was me?"

She giggled. "You have a very distinctive sound to the way you walk."

"Ah, so you've memorized my canter."

She reached for her purse. "That, and your cologne gives you away every time."

I chuckled. "So, any plans for the weekend?"

She stood to her feet. "Not particularly. I'm sure I'll have to field some bullshit with Dad, but other than that, I plan on resting. Yourself?"

"Hopefully, starting my weekend by taking you to coffee?"

Her eyes met mine. "What?"

I straightened my back. "I thought we could make Friday coffee after work a thing we do. We could ride together—or separately—and get some coffee. Maybe a pastry. Just shoot the shit and talk."

She blinked. "You want to get coffee with me again after what happened last week?"

I shrugged. "Why not? It's not your fault coffee went sideways."

She smiled softly. "Yeah, sure. That sounds nice."

I rapped my fingers against her desk. "Wonderful. You want to drive together or separately?"

And that's how we ended up in my truck heading to the same coffee house. We grabbed our coffee, and I had to fight Bella in order to pay for the order. Then, we took a seat at the same table that met a very rough fate last Friday. I eased myself into the chair and saw Bella staring anxiously at the doorway as if her father would be coming in any moment to burst our bubble.

So, I took her hand in mine. "It's okay. Just take a breath."

She drew in a deep one through her nose. "Do you feel like everyone's staring at us?"

I smoothed my thumb against her skin. "No. Do you?"

She nodded. "Yeah. I feel like they're just watching and waiting, you know?"

"I mean, you do look pretty good in that dress. I'd be staring if I weren't already."

Her eyes whipped up to mine. "What?"

I released her hand. "What."

She blinked. "You think I look nice in this?"

I sipped my black coffee. "Of course. You look beautiful in anything you wear."

Her cheeks flushed. "Thank you."

I leaned back. "No thanks needed for the truth."

She cleared her throat. "So, how did your day go? Any news to report?"

I shook my head. "Unfortunately, nothing. Which is rough because I'm awaiting a response from my brothers on a very important email regarding something I feel is critical to the company."

"And none of them have gotten back to you yet?"

I clicked my tongue. "Well, Boone has."

"What did he say?"

I mocked his tone of voice. "Whatever you feel is best, Wyatt."

She giggled. "Is that what he always says or something?"

I crossed my leg over my knee. "It's what I expected. Boone's always been laid back, especially when it comes to the family business. And that doesn't always rub me the right way. But, he's the only one other than myself who doesn't have any family to consult on what I'm asking about, so it doesn't shock me that he's gotten back to me first. I just assumed that a couple of weeks' worth of time would have been enough for my other brothers to discuss it with their partners."

"Care to tell me what you guys are discussing?"

"Unfortunately, I can't. Not until I have them all on board for it. But don't worry, it only affects the board of investors and us. Everyone's jobs will still be intact."

She blinked. "You want to buy them out, don't you?"

I paused. "Well. I didn't expect you to put that together so easily."

She snickered. "I'm not an idiot, Wyatt. I know how to put pieces of a puzzle in place."

And out of nowhere, Bryce's voice sounded behind me. "Yeah, Wyatt. She's not an idiot."

A smile spread across my cheeks. "Have you come to talk to me in person about that email?"

Bryce pulled up a chair beside me. "No, I haven't. Willow and I are still crunching some numbers, and she's going to go talk to a fiduciary today to make sure it's something we can feasibly do."

I nodded slowly. "So, that means you'll have an answer for me this evening?"

He rolled his eyes. "We'll have an answer for you when we have an answer for you."

Bella smiled. "Yeah, Wyatt. He'll have an answer for you when he's got it, duh."

Bryce barked with laughter. "So, you must be the girl who has my brother here so distracted."

Bella's eyes widened, and my head fell back.

"For real, man?"

Bryce patted my shoulder. "I'm telling you, I haven't seen him this distracted, well, ever."

Bella blushed. "I didn't mean to impede."

I rolled my eyes. "Don't you have horses to train or something?"

Bryce chuckled. "And I love that he isn't denying it, either."

Bella joined him in the joke, but I didn't think it was very funny.

"Got your sugar-laced coffee, sweetheart," Willow said.

I looked up at the sound of her voice. "I thought you were at a fiduciary?"

Willow pulled up a chair next to Bella. "Just got done. I was only across the street."

I smirked. "So, how did it go?"

Bryce held out his hand. "Don't answer that until we have a chance to talk."

Willow smiled. "Bryce is right. He and I need to talk first, but let's just say it's the first step in what is hopefully a series of steps that lead to good news."

I held out my hand. "See? She's on board. Why can't you be on board?"

Bryce threw his hands into the air. "I never said I wasn't on board! But, I've got a family to provide for, and I can't throw our financial goals under the bus for something like this. What you want to do is massive, and it's going to take time."

Bella sipped her coffee. "Especially if you want to buy them all out at once. I could understand the need to go-go-go if you want to buy them out individually so as not to tank your stock in the market, but if you want to go full force and do it all at once, it needs to be carefully planned so your stock doesn't take such a hit."

Bryce held out his hand toward her. "See? She gets it."

Willow's eyebrows rose. "How do you know all of that?"

Bella giggled. "I got my degree in business."

Bryce smiled brightly. "She should be helping us run this company, then. She knows more than she's letting on."

I nodded. "Ryan made an excellent choice with her, that's for sure."

Bella leaned forward. "Speaking of Ryan, how is he doing? I think someone said something about paternity leave?"

Bryce took a long pull from his cold coffee. "He's doing

great. His girlfriend, Ellie, has a son named Micah. And from what I hear, Micah has been all too eager to help out where he can."

Willow giggled. "Get this: Ellie called me a few days ago and said she woke up to Micah and Ryan cooking breakfast. He was showing Micah how to flip pancakes."

Bella's face softened. "Awww! That's so cute! Isn't that cute, Wyatt?"

I folded my hands against my thigh. "Very cute, actually. It's good to hear that they're doing well."

Bryce pinned me with a look. "You aren't bothering him with work shit, are you?"

Bella crooked an eyebrow. "Or hounding him about this email?"

Willow clapped her hands as she laughed. "The girl's already catching on! I like her, Wyatt. Don't screw up whatever this is."

My eyes found Bella's. "Whatever this is, trust me. I'm trying not to."

"Hey!" Bart exclaimed. "Look who's here!"

Bryce craned his neck. "Bart! Luna! Over here! We've got room for a couple more seats."

Bella scooted over. "Luna, you can sit by me."

I snagged a chair from the table behind me. "Come here, Bart. I want to talk to you."

Bryce glared playfully at me. "And not about the email."

Bart trotted over. "Actually, Luna and I were going to call you tonight, but I guess now is as good of a time as any."

I smiled. "As good of a time as any for what?"

Luna peered over his shoulder with two small coffees. "We're in."

I clapped my hands. "Yes! See? It's not so hard, Bryce."

Everyone fell apart in laughter as my brother glared at me. I blew him a kiss before picking up my coffee and taking a long swig of it. And as we all settled down at the table, I noticed something. I noticed how well Bella fit in with all of us with ease.

I wonder if Dad would like her.

"Ah, see! Look at that smile," Bart said.

Bella giggled. "You okay there, Wyatt?"

I blinked rapidly to pull myself out of my trance. "What? What's happening?"

Everyone at the table roared with laughter as I searched Bella's eyes.

"You were staring," she said.

Electricity shot through my veins. "My apologies."

She shook her head. "No, no, you're fine. I promise."

My eyes held hers, and my heart stopped in my chest. What the fuck had this woman done to me? I mean, I'd only known her for... what? Two weeks? And she already had me captivated?

How could I feel like this for someone after only fourteen days?

Is this how Ryan felt for Ellie?

I felt myself smiling harder as my eyes danced along Bella's gorgeous features. Her pouty lower lip upturned into a smile that stole my breath. Her presence blanketed me in a comforting warmth I usually had to provide for myself. And as I gazed into her sparkling eyes, a shocking thought crossed my mind.

I could look into your eyes for the rest of my life.

"So! Bella. How are you liking working at the new headquarters?" Bryce asked.

Bella nodded as she reached for her pastry. "It's going really well."

Bart patted my back. "Wyatt here not breathing down your neck too much?"

Bella grinned. "Just enough to keep me on my toes."

The guys chuckled and kept giving me those atta-boy eyes, but I didn't pay them any mind. Whatever it was that was blossoming between Bella and me could go at its own pace.

Especially if it meant that we had a higher chance of being successful at, well, whatever *this* was.

Luna sighed with content. "We need to do this more often."

Willow furrowed her brow. "What? Getting together for coffee?"

Bella shrugged. "How about getting together, in general?"

Willow pointed at her. "I like that idea better."

Luna turned to face her. "Got any plans for this weekend?"

And as the girls started making plans together as if they'd known one another for years, I felt something in my soul slide into place, like a puzzle piece finding the right hole. Bella's smile lit up the room, and her laughter washed over me like warm, summertime ocean waves.

Then, after the girls finalized their Saturday evening plans, we all got up to disperse.

Bella's hand slipped into mine as we walked back out to my truck.

🦊 17 🦊

Bella

"I had a great time at coffee," I said.

Wyatt grinned as we stood next to my company car. "I'm glad. I enjoyed it, as well."

"But, were you serious about making this a regular thing for us? I mean, a regular Friday afternoon thing?"

He nodded. "I was, yes. I still am."

I smiled softly. "Then, I'm looking forward to next Friday."

His intense gaze held mine. "As am I."

I wanted him to kiss me. Everything inside of me screamed for him to kiss me. But instead, he bowed his head and turned to walk back to his truck. I was disappointed, sure. However, it was a gentleman's move not to kiss me after having such a rocky start. And yeah, we hadn't talked about what had happened between us in the field—twice or how we had fallen asleep in one another's arms in the bed of his truck. Did we have to talk about it and spoil it, though?

I kind of enjoyed having a little secret like that just between the two of us.

"Come on, Bella. Get a move on," I murmured to myself.

I unlocked my car and slipped inside, but I couldn't help myself. I followed Wyatt in the rearview mirror with my eyes and quickly noticed that he wasn't getting into his truck. He leaned in through the passenger's side to retrieve his briefcase. Then I watched with a curious stare as he made his way back inside the building.

Does he always work so late?

An idea popped into my head, but I had to make sure to play my cards right. I turned over the engine and raced back home, only to find Mom cooking up a storm in the kitchen like she normally did. Dad's snores filled the living room, following me around the house as if he were perched in a corner and watching my every move. I didn't let it deter me, though.

"That you, Bella?" Mom asked.

I quickly kissed her on the cheek. "I just wanted to let you know that I won't be home for dinner tonight."

Mom cleared her throat. "Well, don't let your father know you're going out with that Wyatt boy again."

I rolled my eyes and kept my mouth shut as I started pulling out Tupperware containers. I packed up two portions of Mom's cooking and made sure to slice off two slices of dessert from the red velvet cake taunting me on the island of the kitchen. I grabbed a couple of bottles of water and filled up two tumblers full of Mom's ultra-perfect sweet tea.

Then, with Dad still snoring on the couch, I kissed Mom's cheek one last time before heading out.

As I made my way back toward work, I drew in deep breaths. I prayed I wouldn't be an intrusion or an unwelcome guest as I parked my car and gathered up everything I had fetched for us. I used my keycard to get into the building and made a beeline for the elevator, wondering if Wyatt already knew I was inside. I mean, I didn't know who got what information whenever someone swiped their card, so as far as I was concerned, he might have already received an alert to the fact that I was back.

Maybe he'll be just as happy to see me as I will be to see him.

I knew I had only been away from his side for about an hour, but to me, it felt like an eternity. I felt that voice in my head, chirping at me about making a mistake. About the things I could lose if a relationship with my boss went south. I shoved it all to the side, though, when the elevator dumped me out onto the top floor. I carried everything toward the black door at the end of the hallway and paused to shift everything in my arms.

But, Wyatt's voice answered the question I had before. "Come on in, Bella. Door's open."

I giggled as I pushed my way inside. "So, you get notifications whenever someone swipes their card?"

He didn't look up from his paperwork. "Yes."

I eased the door closed behind me. "You hungry? I brought food."

He pointed to the chair in front of his desk. "Take a seat. I'm almost done with this folder."

It all seemed so formal, but I tried not to let it get to me. I walked over and set the Tupperware and the drinks onto the edge of his desk before sitting down and taking a load off. I studied Wyatt and the languid way his hand scribbled across the papers in front of him. How his long, dexterous fingers gripped his pen, flexing his knuckles and causing the veins in his forearms to bulge a bit. He had his coat off and his sleeves rolled up, exposing just enough skin to make my nipples pucker against the fabric of my bra.

Then, he set his pen down and lifted his gaze to my face. "Thank you for dinner; it is much appreciated."

And to my shock, he turned to his computer and started typing.

I didn't let it deter me, though. "Mind if I eat with you? I'm kind of starving."

He nodded. "Help yourself."

I plucked through the Tupperware containers before choosing a bottle of water as my drink. I scooted the rest of it a bit closer to Wyatt, hoping to break his trance long enough to get him to eat with me. But, he kept typing away at his desk as if I weren't even there.

I took a bite of my food. "Anything I can help with?"

He sighed and finally paused his movements. "What are you doing here, Bella?"

I paused my chewing. "Hanging out on a Friday night. What else?"

His eye twitched. "Didn't you make plans with the girls or something?"

"For tomorrow night, sure. But, you already know that because you were there when we made plans."

His eye twitched again. "When you finish eating, you can exit the same way you came."

"Oh, no. See, that's where you're wrong. I don't know how much time after hours you spend up here working away, but I'm not leaving until I know you've eaten dinner. You can't be productive without energy, and you get that energy from food. So, unless you want me sitting here all night with you, I suggest you pause for a moment and eat."

I saw the shadow of a grin playing across his cheeks as he stopped typing. "So, theoretically, if I didn't want you to leave, then all I have to do is not eat."

I blinked. "Or, you could simply ask me to stay. That works, too."

He finally turned to face me. "It does smell good."

I smirked. "My mother is a fabulous cook. She's always had that going for her."

He pointed to the red tumbler I brought. "Tea?"

I nodded. "Have at it. The blue one's mine. I already took a sip out of it in the car on the way here."

He scooped up the tumbler. "I love a good sweet tea."

His swig of tea turned into a few bites of food, and soon the two of us were talking back and forth as if he weren't in the middle of some random night shift in his office. We stuffed ourselves silly before we even got to the cake. And when it was time to dig into dessert, he took the Tupperware and walked over to what looked like a wall full of drawers. I watched him carefully as he swung open a small wooden door, revealing a microwave behind it.

And after warming our cake up just a tad, he pulled up a chair beside me to sit instead of going back around to his office chair.

"My compliments to the chef," he said through his first bite of cake.

I smiled. "I'll let Mom know you enjoyed it."

He took another massive bite. "Did she bake this, too?"

I nodded. "Mhm. I learned everything I know about cooking and baking from her."

He shook his head slowly. "You're going to ruin me with this kind of thing. You know that, right?"

I giggled. "If by 'ruined' you mean 'spoil' then, the honor is all mine. You work much too hard and put up with too much shit not to be."

I felt his eyes studying my face. "You're something else; you know that?"

My eyes fluttered up to his. "Not particularly."

His gaze held my stare, and I felt that tell-tale heat in my pelvis again. It trickled up to my hips and tainted my spine, causing me to shiver in my seat. I turned my attention back to my cake, trying to keep my emotions and feelings at bay. But, when Wyatt scooted his chair closer to me, I felt our knees fall together, and my breath caught in my throat.

"Bella."

I dropped my eyes to my dessert and took the last bite of my cake. "Yeah?"

"Look at me."

I swallowed hard and did as he asked. "What's up?"

He set his half-eaten cake off to the side before standing to his feet. He took everything out of my hands and plucked my bottled water from between my thighs, setting it all onto the edge of his desk. My eyes slowly caressed his body from his knees to his forehead. The cream-colored suit he donned looked spectacular on him, especially with the royal blue button-front shirt he had paired with it. I wondered if the man's closet was full of nothing but suits explicitly tailored for his wondrous body. I felt my cheeks heating as I thought about the beautifully etched muscles beneath the clothes that separated us. Then, he held out his hand in silence.

"What?" I asked.

He grinned at me as he wiggled his fingers.

"What are you going to do?" I asked breathlessly.

He chuckled. "Why don't you take my hand and find out?"

My stomach sank to my toes. My heart leaped into my throat. And as my hand moved, like it had a mind of its own, I felt my knees bending and my calves contracting. My core tightened as my hand slid against Wyatt's, clinging to him as I stood to my feet. I felt him guiding me to his body, his leg sliding between my thighs.

And as my cheeks heated with a need for him, I lost myself in the constant intensity of his gaze.

"Care to dance?" Wyatt asked.

My jaw dropped open in shock as he held my hand within his. He raised them both, suspending them in midair as his free arm wrapped around the small of my back. I felt his cock pressed against my core and his strong abs pressed against my soft stomach. I had the urge to lean my head against his chest, so I did, and when he started swaying, I could've sworn I heard humming pouring from his lips.

Yes, humming.

Wyatt was singing a song for us to dance to.

I'm a goner.

Shock didn't even begin to describe what wafted through my system. The tenderness with which Wyatt cradled me was so unlike him. The softness of his humming and the fluidness of the notes was something I would have never expected of him. And the way he held my body against his made me almost feel like he never wanted to let me go.

Why did this man have to be my boss?

Around and around and around we spun, rocking softly, side to side. I closed my eyes and allowed myself to be swept away as thoughts of my father and my mother's warning faded effortlessly into the background. I drew in deep breaths of his cologne as he led me around his office, giving me a silent, guided tour I didn't give a shit about.

It wasn't until I felt my back fall against his bookshelf, though, that I pulled myself from my trance.

"Wyatt?" I whispered.

He gripped my chin. "You look beautiful in the moonlight; you know that?"

My eyes rose to his lips. "So do you."

And when I watched his lips come closer to mine, I let my eyes fall closed once more, accepting what was about to happen between the two of us without a second thought given to the consequences.

You can have all of me, Wyatt.

I just hoped I wasn't making the wrong decision in all of this.

❧ 18 ❧

Wyatt

I restrained myself long enough to memorize the way our lips connected. The way her tongue slid effortlessly into my mouth. Feeling her soft body pressed against my bookshelf stiffened my cock against my pants. But, there was something more than that.

A tingle that worked its way throughout my muscles. As if they were crying out for heaven itself.

It didn't last long, though. I had no self-control when it came to this woman. I didn't know what she held over me that put me into a trance every time she was around, but I never wanted it to stop. I slid my arm around the small of her back and hoisted her into the air, carrying her with just one arm as she giggled against my lips. I walked her back over to my desk. I set her on her feet.

And after pulling away from our kiss for a brief moment, I swiped my arms over my desk.

"Wyatt! Your computer!"

Everything crashed to the floor, and I felt more powerful than I'd ever felt in my entire life. I grabbed her arm and pulled her back to me, colliding our lips as I sucked on her tongue. She melted against me as the heat of her pussy blanketed my clothed cock. And as a deep, dark, resonating need to have her rose within me, my hands found their way to her hips before I spun her around.

"I want you to keep wearing dresses, you hear me?" I growled.

I pressed her face against my desk and ground my cock against her ass cheeks.

"Do you hear me?" I exclaimed.

She whimpered. "Yes, Mr. Remington. I hear you loud and clear."

I growled. "What did you call me?"

"M—Mr. Remington, sir?"

I bent forward and nipped at the shell of her ear. "And don't you ever forget it."

Up went her dress, over went her panties, and out came my cock. I held my breath as I entered her, relishing the wetness already apparent for me. She moaned out into my office, filling it with her scent as I straightened my back. Then, I fisted her hair and started pounding against her.

"Holy shit," she hissed.

I watched her ass cheeks jiggle for me. "My God, you're perfection."

My balls were already pulling up, but I refused to come. Not yet. Not when I needed to feel Bella tremble against me. The way she sounded when she orgasmed had fully etched itself into my memory, haunting my dreams whenever I wasn't with her. Even in the quiet of my office, every once in a while, I swore I heard her. Moaning my name and gasping for more while my hands tried their most diligent to keep on task.

I'd never masturbated in my office until she came along. But dammit, I loved every second of it.

"Wyatt! Yes!"

I panted for air. "Come for me. Now. Drench me, Bella."

She whimpered. "Oh, Wyatt. Oh, yeah."

I stuffed her full of my cock and drew in a sobering breath as her pussy collapsed around me. I'd never had a woman squeeze me as tight as she did, and I almost came right then and there. Her heat was too much. The wet sounds her pussy made every time I filled her made my mouth salivate for more. I felt like a wild animal who had finally found his first—and last—meal.

But, I wasn't done with her yet.

I ripped my cock out from between her legs and pulled her up by her hair. I turned her around and wrapped my arms around her, cradling her weak body against my own. I bent down and picked her up, gingerly placing her back against my bare desk. And as I gazed down into her eyes, her legs locked around me.

"Wyatt?"

I kissed the top of her nose. "Yes, Bella?"

She shook her head softly. "What in the world are we doing?"

I slid my cock back into her body without resistance. "Enjoying the time we have together."

Her eyes fluttered closed, and I slowed my movements. I wanted to feel every slope of her body move against me as we rocked in tandem with one another. With every thrust, she pulled me closer. Deeper. Farther into her body. In her arms, I was incapable of doing wrong. In her eyes, I was incapable of doing harm.

And when I was with her, I was like the man I wanted to be.

"Oh, Bella," I groaned.

I captured her lips and swallowed her sounds as our movements grew desperate. The sloshing sounds between us that ricocheted up to my ears made my cock twitch with a need for release. Her hands slid through my hair. She gripped my suit jacket in an effort to pull me even closer. I had no idea where the fuck my body ended and hers began, but I had no plans to unravel us anytime soon.

But, my dick had other plans.

"Oh, shit. Bella, I'm coming. I'm coming. Holy fuck."

She bucked deeply against me. "I'm so close. So close. Don't stop."

I sank my teeth against her neck. "Holy shit, you're fantastic."

Then, her back arched. "Yes, Wyatt. Right there!"

I rutted against her as my hips stuttered. My arousal shot from my tip as it coated her walls. And just as my body relaxed against hers, I felt her muscles tense. Her fingertips dug into my back, and she trembled against me as she choked out my name, spiraling beneath me with a beauty I'd never witnessed in all my life.

I couldn't stop watching her as she collapsed against my desk, completely spent from our aerobics. Yet still, I wanted more.

I could do this with her for the rest of my life.

"What was that?" Bella asked.

I blinked lazily. "What was what?"

Then, I heard it.

The sound of footsteps coming down the hallway.

"Bella!"

My eyes widened at the sound of her father's voice.

"Bella, dammit! Are you up here?"

"Shit," she hissed.

She pushed me off her with a strength that shocked even me. I stumbled backward, my limp dick swinging between my soaked thighs as her father's footsteps grew closer. How the fuck he managed to get into the building, I didn't know. But, if I found out that someone was here and they had let him in after hours, I'd have their goddamn job. Bella and I rushed to get our clothes situated. I stuffed my cock back into my boxers as she fluffed her hair out. She plucked a few tissues from the box off the floor and wiped at the insides of her knees, and only for a brief moment did I allow myself to take pride in how wet I made her before my office door burst open.

"You," her father glowered.

I stepped in front of Bella and slid my hands into my pockets. "My apologies, Mr. Lancaster. But, only employees are allowed to be here after hours."

He pointed at me. "Give me my daughter. The two of us are going home."

Bella's voice rose behind me. "No, I'm not."

Her father froze. "What did you just say to me?"

She stepped over to my left before she stood beside me. "I'm not leaving with you. Wyatt and I are in the middle of—"

Her father cut her off. "I know exactly what you're in the middle of, and I won't allow it. I won't stand for it. Not in my house!"

I tilted my head. "Please don't make me call security. I'd hate to have you banned from the premises."

He walked up to me and stood so close that I smelled the residual booze on his breath. "You won't lay another fucking finger on my daughter, you slimy son of a bitch. You hear me?"

"That's enough," Bella hissed. And this time, she stepped in front of me and pushed her father back a few steps. "I've had enough of your antics and enough of your bullshit and enough of your hatred to last me a lifetime, Dad. Enough is enough."

He glared at her. "Don't you cuss at me, girl. Remember whose house you live in."

She raised her head high. "And remember why I moved back in the first place."

Silence blanketed my office as I cleared my throat. But, Bella raised her hand to stop me in my tracks before she continued.

"Wyatt is a wonderful man. He's headstrong and confident. He's intelligent and capable. By all accounts, he's the kind of man you should want me with. And yet, you let your hatred from one moment in your life rule over this entire family. I'm not letting that happen anymore, though. I won't let you continue to barge into my work like you own the rights to me any longer."

Her father's face turned red with anger. "And what are you going to do if I don't stop?"

She took a step toward him. "For starters, I'll move out and take my paycheck with me."

His eyes raked along her body. "We didn't need your money beforehand, and we don't need it now."

She snickered. "That's not what all of the past due bills on the kitchen table say."

He pointed at her. "Don't you dare go into our private shit in front of this sorry excuse for a—"

"For a what, Dad? Go ahead. Finish that sentence and I'll make sure you're banned from the premises. Because let me tell you something. If having you arrested and thrown into jail is what it'll take to sober you up and rip you out of a past that you keep clinging to, then so help me God, I'll make sure it happens."

I was utterly floored. I kept watching the two of them go back and forth, and the entire time I only thought about one thing—I'd never had anyone stand up for me like that. Bella and her father kept fighting back and forth, and every time he attempted to attack this company or me, Bella stood on my side of the line.

The moment was short-lived, though.

"Maybe your mother can talk some sense into you, but I'm done," her father growled.

And when I saw him yank her by the arm, I snapped.

I charged Mr. Lancaster and knocked his arm away from Bella. I wrapped my fist up in his stained shirt, barreling him away from her until his back slammed against my book-shelves. Books of all shapes and colors came tumbling down to the floor as I slid him upward, picking him clear up off his goddamn feet.

My vision dripped with red as anger flooded my words. "Don't you ever lay a hand on her again. Ever. Or I'll see to it personally that you spend the rest of your sorry, alcoholic days behind bars. Understood?"

"Stop it!" Bella shrieked.

The sound ripped me from my trance, and I instantly dropped her father. He collapsed into a heap, panting for air he hadn't worked for as I stepped back a few feet. I slid my hands down my button-front shirt before I cleared my throat, blinking away the rest of the red that clouded my vision. Then, I turned to Bella. "My apologies."

She shook her head. "You're not the one who owes anyone here an apology."

Her father struggled to get up, and at one point in time, he even reached out for Bella. But she didn't budge. She watched him struggle to get up before he eventually pulled himself upright with the bookshelves adhered to my wall. And the entire time, the word "security" was balanced on the tip of my tongue. If he made another move toward her, I'd have him hauled out of here in handcuffs. I already had half a mind to put him on the ban list permanently just to have the satisfaction of seeing him arrested one day.

I was quickly getting the idea that as long as Bella worked here, he'd be a constant nuisance.

"Your daughter deserves better, you know," I said.

Mr. Lancaster's eyes slid up and down my body. "You'd do well to remember that, too."

Bella sighed. "Come on, Dad. Did you catch an Uber?"

He shook his head. "Your mother's out front."

I saw something pass behind Bella's eyes, and I could've sworn it was defeat. It killed me inside to know she felt so helpless while trying to do the best for her ungrateful family.

"Would you like me to escort you out?" I asked.

"No," her father said.

Bella snickered as she held my gaze. "He wasn't asking you, Dad. Shut up."

I grinned. "Nice."

She smiled softly. "I had a really nice time. Thank you."

I shook my head. "No, no. Thank you for bringing me dinner. I probably wouldn't have eaten had you not brought it over."

"That's what I'm here for."

Her father groaned. "You two through?"

"Shut up," we both said in unison.

I wanted to cross the room and hug her, but I resisted the urge. I held her lingering eyes for a few more seconds before she cleared her throat and turned her attention to her father. She gathered up the empty Tupperware containers and half-guzzled tumblers of tea. Then, once she was packed up, she started walking toward my office door.

"You coming or what, Dad?" she asked flatly.

Mr. Lancaster shot me one last look that could've killed if looks had that kind of power. Then, the two of them exited my office. I clasped my hands behind my back and waited until I heard the ding of the elevator, followed by the almost-muted whir that meant they were headed back down to the main lobby.

Then, I charged my bookshelf.

"Son of a bitch!"

I ripped the rest of the books out of their places and listened as they tumbled to the floor.

"What a fucking bastard!"

I stormed over to my stuff on the floor and started kicking it around.

"Bella. Deserves. More than this!"

And after punching my fist straight through my office wall, my anger finally ebb away. I pulled back my hand and found my knuckles bleeding, which only added to my frustration. I needed to calm down. I needed to go on a drive. But, I knew that if I got into the car, I wouldn't stop until I got to Bella's house.

So, I stormed out of my office with my bleeding knuckles and headed across the street.

Because I needed a fucking drink.

🏵 19 🏵

Bella

"Bella, I'm sorry. You know how your father can be sometimes."

I ignored my mother's pleas as I helped my father up the steps.

"At least you've learned your lesson," he murmured.

Yeah, and you're about to learn yours.

Somehow, I exercised enough restraint to keep my mouth shut. Somehow, I didn't cuss my mother out for being so damn weak as I hauled my father's hungover ass up the steps. Somehow, I managed not to slam his head against a wall every time he made some snarky comment.

And when I poured his ass into the tub, I turned on the cold water.

"Holy shit, are you insane?" he exclaimed.

I watched him struggle to get out of the tub. He kept flailing around as if he'd slipped on some ice and couldn't get himself back up again. I wanted to cry. I wanted to scream. I wanted to curse and throw shit and yell at him. But, the coolness and collectedness of my anger told me exactly the point I had hit.

It was time to give my father an ultimatum.

"God... dammit!" he roared.

I reached over and turned on the hot water to rid him of his momentary misery before I leaned against the bathroom counter.

"I'm going to stand right here and wait until you calm down. Then, I'm going to speak. And for every moment you interrupt me, that's one more date I'm going on with Wyatt."

He gritted his teeth. "Over my dead body."

"Trust me, your drinking already has you halfway there."

He stopped struggling and sank deeper into the warm bathwater. "I know you'll never see things my way, but I'm protecting you."

I shook my head. "No, Dad. If anything, you're the only person in my life hurting me."

His eyes shot up to mine. "I'm doing no such thing."

I shrugged. "You don't get to charge into my work and yell at my boss, yank me around by my arm, and attempt to control my love life and then tell me you're not hurting me. You don't get to be an asshole and then tell me how I'm going to feel about it. And before you say anything about my cursing at you, get the hell over it. I'm a grown woman raising an overgrown toddler who won't stop stuffing his face with shit he shouldn't be having. You don't get a say in this until you grow up."

His silence told me I'd struck a nerve, so I capitalized on the moment.

"Dad, do you have any idea what you've done to our family? The depths you've sunk to in order to make us all miserable just because you can't find your own happiness? I mean, it kills you to see us happy, doesn't it? Because you're not happy?"

His eyes stared straight ahead. "Think whatever you want."

"I don't think. I know. I've watched it my entire life. I've watched Mom carry you on the back of her two jobs she worked before she got injured in the warehouse. I've watched you drink away her disability because you can't even come to terms with the fact that you got knocked off a horse during a rodeo."

He gritted his teeth. "That fucking Remington man knocked me off my horse."

"So, what?"

His eyes snapped up to mine. "What do you mean, so what?"

I narrowed my eyes. "So. What? So, what if you got thrown from a horse? There's a reason why you sign waivers before every rodeo. You knew the risks going in every single time, and you took them anyway. Why in the world are you so shocked that you got hurt?"

"That bastard slammed into my horse and knocked me down. And not once was he penalized!"

"And you think the refs wouldn't have called that if that were true?"

"Well, obviously, he paid them off with all that company money he's got!"

I scoffed. "Or, maybe you just don't like the fact that you were paying more attention to Mr. Remington than you were anything else."

He shook his head. "You can think what you want. I'm done arguing with you."

"Good. Then, maybe I can get back to my life without your constant ungrateful, drunken interference."

He pointed up at me. "You're not seeing that boy under my roof, though. Not happening."

I nodded. "Fair enough. I'll be out by the end of next week."

My dad paused. "What?"

I turned on my feet. "I'll be out by next Friday. Make sure Mom knows."

"Hey! Don't you walk away from me!"

I stopped. "Your regrets aren't going to rob me of my life, Dad. I won't allow it."

His voice softened just a tad. "I'm only trying to protect you."

I slowly turned back around. "From who? It's not like your

issue is with Wyatt. He wasn't the one in that arena with you when you were thrown from your horse. Your issue is with his father."

"My issue is with that whole family. They think they're better than everyone else."

I shrugged. "And maybe that's so. Maybe, deep down, they really do think they're heaven on earth or whatever it is you believe. But, until you can start acting like the level-headed man I once knew you to be, then know this—I'd rather be with them any day than spend one more second of my life battling against you. Because I can't do it anymore, Dad. I can't keep being the parent to my parents."

His eyes turned back toward the wall, but I heard his voice loud and clear. "Do you care about the boy?"

I didn't hesitate. "Very much so."

He sighed. "Where in the world did I go wrong with you?"

I ignored his question. "Finish up your bath. You stink. And just so we're clear: I won't stop seeing Wyatt until he tells me he's done. Not you."

Then, I left Dad to his own devices.

I made my way out of Mom and Dad's bedroom only to find Mom standing in the hallway. She wrung her hands in front of her body and had the guiltiest look on her face. I should've been furious at her, but I honestly understood. When Dad got angry, there was no stopping him. And if you were the one in his way? Then, heaven help you. I knew all she was doing was trying to tame the beast. I knew she was doing her best.

So, I held my arms out for her. "Come here."

She rushed toward me and wrapped me up tightly before she started crying against my shoulder. The sound broke my heart, and I held her as long as she needed me to. I ran my fingers through her hair as she choked out apology after apology. And when she finished, she moved away from me to make her way toward the bedroom.

But, I caught her arm. "Mom."

She sighed. "Your daddy needs help, sweetheart. I can't just leave him in there to drown himself in a tub."

I slowly turned her around. "He's a grown man who's made his decisions in life. It's time for him to start reaping the consequences of those decisions and pulling himself up out of the hole he's dug for himself."

Her watery eyes met mine. "I can't just leave him there."

"You're not leaving him, Mom. By doing nothing, you're doing the best thing for him there is. We can't keep picking him up anymore. We can't keep lugging him around. Doing that cost you your ability to work. Don't you think that's enough?"

Her lower lip quivered. "How did it get this bad, Bella?"

I pulled her back into my arms. "I don't know, Mom. I just don't know."

I'd never heard my mother cry like that in all my life. But, as I held her against my body, I felt her shivering with each sob that fell from her lips. I couldn't imagine the life Mom had led because of all of this. I couldn't imagine watching my soulmate fall into the depths of despair and be helpless to stop it. I couldn't imagine taking wedding vows that said, "for better or for worse," and then having that "worse" take over my life.

My mother was the strongest person I knew, and she deserved better than this.

"Come on, let's go downstairs and make some coffee," I whispered.

She drew in a broken breath. "We should pour Dad's alcohol down the sink, too."

I blinked. "Wait, really?"

She took a step back and nodded. "Yeah. I know where he keeps all of the hidden half-bottles of whiskey around here. It's time we put our foot down."

I smiled softly. "Yes, it's about time."

I followed my mother downstairs and put on a pot of coffee. Then, one by one, we emptied Dad's shelf in the pantry. We uncorked bottles and listened as the sink guzzled them down. Mom walked me around the house and showed me all of the nooks and crannies where Dad kept everything from airplane bottles of liquor to full-sized bottles of vodka. We unscrewed every cap and uncorked every bottle of wine before holding it over the sink. We washed it down with plenty of water so no one could smell the alcohol wafting up the drain, then tossed the last of the bottles into a new trash bag.

Mom tied up the strings and took it out to the garbage can just as the coffee pot went off.

So, I fixed us each a cup and had it waiting for her when she came back inside.

"How angry do you think he's going to be?" she asked.

I sipped my drink. "Pretty angry."

She nodded slowly. "You think we should leave and have him deal with it on his own?"

I giggled. "Who are you, and what have you done to my mother?"

She smiled sadly. "Are you really going to move out?"

I blinked. "You heard that, huh?"

She smirked. "You bellow like your father. It was impossible not to."

I leaned back in my chair. "Part of me wants to."

"Part of me is inclined to agree with you."

"And I really should be living on my own."

She nodded slowly. "Yes, you should."

I eyed her carefully. "How will you and Dad pay the bills, though?"

She shrugged. "All I have to do is take him off the account, and he won't be able to access my disability. Then, we can pay bills just fine."

"You get unemployment, too, right?"

"It kicked in about a year ago, yeah. Took a lot of fighting to get that money, though. But, if we can really nip your father's drinking in the bud, we'll be good to go. His drinking is what's been doing us in for so long."

I cocked my head. "Can I ask why you haven't put your foot down with him until now? Because I can't imagine living with that kind of horror day in and day out."

"Honestly?"

"For once, yes."

She snickered softly. "I've been afraid of him."

My heart broke for her. "Oh, Mom."

She waved her hand in the air. "Don't 'oh, Mom' me. I made my bed. I chose my path. And when your father needed me to step in right at the beginning, I chose not to. I kept telling myself that he was a grown man and that he didn't need my help. But, he did."

"So, you're punishing yourself."

She shrugged. "Can't say I don't deserve it, can you?"

I leaned forward and held her gaze. "You don't deserve it, Mom. Neither of us does."

The whooshing sound of water above our heads startled us from our conversation. Dad had unplugged the bathtub, which meant he'd be doing one of two things. He'd come down here to find us, or he'd stumble his ass into bed. I heard him plodding around and grumbling to himself, courtesy of the very thin walls in the house. I reached for my coffee and braced myself as his footsteps migrated toward the stairs.

But then, the sounds ceased.

"He's standing at the top to listen," Mom whispered.

I furrowed my brow, continuing to whisper, "Does he do that often?"

"Unfortunately. It's how he knows so much."

Finally, after a few minutes of dead quiet, Dad backtracked into the bedroom. The door slammed, and he started cursing to himself; instinctively, Mom got up. I took her hand, though. I eased her back down into her chair. She was itching to go up there and help him. I knew she wanted to smooth things over and get back to business as usual. We couldn't keep going like this, though. Our family would implode if something didn't change and quickly.

Then, just as Dad tumbled into bed, a knock came at the front door, causing me to put my coffee down and stand to my feet.

❦ 20 ❧

Wyatt

"Girl trouble, or work trouble?" Boone's voice sounded behind me, and I sighed.

"Work."

He sat at the bar next to me. "Girl troubles; got it."

I rolled my eyes. "Boone, I'm really not in the mood t—"

He pointed at the bartender. "I'll have one of whatever this guy's had up until now. Thank you."

I clicked my tongue. "What if I'm four shots and two margaritas in?"

He chuckled. "One, you don't take shots. And two, you hate lime."

I threw back the rest of my whiskey neat. "Whatever."

I watched the bartender set two whiskey neats in front of

Boone, and he threw them back effortlessly. My younger brother had always been a partier. I'd never known him to stay with one girl for more than a month or so, and every time we turned around, he was gushing about another blonde with fake tits and too much makeup who sucked cock like a champ. And there, for a while, we rivaled one another. Jumping from girl to girl as if they were going out of fashion.

I had no passion for leading that life anymore, though.

"Another one?" the bartender asked.

"Just a water, thanks," I murmured.

Boone clapped my back with his hand. "Hey, don't stop on my account. Because I'm definitely having at least two more."

I sighed. "I figured as much."

He smacked his lips. "So, tell me about the problem."

"Even if there were a problem, you'd be the last person—"

He spun my chair in his direction. "You can talk, or you can drink. And if you aren't going to drink, then you're going to talk."

I blinked. "And if I don't do either?"

He shrugged. "You're picking up the tab, and I'm about to treat everyone in here to three drinks of their choice."

I groaned. "Fine, all right. Yes, it's girl troubles."

The bartender slid me a glass of water, and I caught it before he set another drink in front of Boone.

"What kicked up the troubles?" he asked.

I turned to face the bar once more. "Her drunk father."

"Ah, the dads. They're a hard bunch, aren't they?"

"He's stormed into work countless times now, including tonight."

He paused. "Why would some girl's dad storm into the headquarters?"

I sipped my water. "Because the girl is Bella."

"Who's that?"

I rolled my eyes. "The new front desk secretary."

He barked with laughter. "No, shit! You're bangin' the new secretary?"

I shot him a look. "You better watch your next words carefully."

His eyebrows rose. "Whoa, now. What was that all about?"

I turned my eyes forward again. "Bella deserves your respect. I expect you to make sure it's given from your end."

"Wow. You're serious about this girl, aren't you?"

I took another sip of my water. "Yeah. I am."

"Then, what the fuck are you doing sitting here?"

"What?"

He turned my chair back in his direction. "Wyatt. What the fuck are you doing sitting here, drowning yourself in the same shit her father is when you could be out there, scooping her back up off your feet?"

He's got a point. "Just needed to deal with my anger in a way that didn't put another hole in my office wall."

Boone blinked. "So... there's already a hole in your office wall?"

I sighed. "Yep."

He nodded. "Well, if I were in your shoes—and I hope never to be because fuck love and all that shit—but you should get the hell out of here and go find her if it's that serious. Drinking ain't gonna solve shit."

"Says the guy who goes out every weekend and twice on Wednesdays."

"One, that sounds like a great new Wednesday tradition. And two, if you don't want to end up like me, then don't make the same mistakes." He had a point.

"Bartender?"

"Yep?"

"I'd like to cash out, please. You can put it on Boone's tab."

My brother chuckled. "I see how you're gonna do me. All right, all right. But, just this once."

I grinned. "See ya."

"Good luck sweeping her off her feet!"

After heading back across the street to lock up the building for the night, I raced back down to my vehicle. I tossed my briefcase into the bed of my truck and wrangled my jacket on before I hopped into the driver's seat. I cranked the engine and didn't even bother buckling my seatbelt as I drove all the way out to Bella's place.

Then, after taking a deep breath in, I knocked on her front door.

Deep breaths. In and out. You're not drunk. You're not her father. You're not—

"Wyatt?" Her incredible voice pulled me from the depths of my mind.

"Hey, Bella."

She wrinkled her nose. "Is that whiskey on your breath?"

I slid my hands into my pockets. "I'm not drunk, I swear. I just needed a way to wind down after things happened in my office, and you were sort of indisposed."

She blushed. "It did get a bit out of hand, didn't it?"

"A little bit, which is actually why I've stopped by."

She peeked over her shoulder. "This really isn't a good time. Can we do this—"

"It'll only take a couple of minutes, max. I promise."

She licked her lips before she stepped outside, closing the door behind her. "All right, but make it quick."

So, I launched into the apology I kept rehearsing in my mind. "Bella, I'm sorry for the way I let my anger spiral out of control. I should've been the bigger man and kept control of things since I didn't have any biological reason to let loose. You deserved better than what happened tonight, and all I've wanted to make sure of is that you get it. Some of the things I said to your father were completely uncalled for and very disrespectful, despite the disrespect he's shown to both of us. I don't want to be like him, and I don't want to be equated with him. All I want is to make sure you have everything you could possibly need, and I'm sorry for not showing you that this evening."

Her eyes stayed locked with mine for the entire apology. She didn't interrupt me, she didn't overwrite me, and she didn't try to shut me up. But, the second my lips were done moving, she threw herself at me. She wrapped her arms around my neck—much to my surprise—and pressed her lips against mine.

And the feeling of her tongue caressing my own as she pushed her way into my mouth made me growl. "Oh, Bella," I mumbled against her lips.

She whimpered down the back of my throat, and my arms tightened around her waist. I resisted the urge to pick her up and take her back to my truck because I knew if I left here with her, I'd never bring her back. I'd take her to my place, settle her into my bed, and I'd tell her we'd get her things in the morning.

Because dammit, I wanted her at my side for the rest of my fucking life.

"Ahem."

Bella squeaked before she jumped away from me, and I drew in a quick breath through my nose. The voice that sounded beside me was delicate, and when I turned to face the doorway, I found the spitting image of Bella standing there.

Bella giggled. "Wyatt, this is my mother. Mom, this is Wyatt Remington."

She held out her hand. "The pleasure's all mine."

I shook her hand delicately. "Took the words right out of my mouth, Mrs. Lancaster."

She dropped my hand. "Come on in. Bella just put on some coffee, and I've got red velvet cake."

I grinned. "I'd love another slice of it. The first one simply wasn't enough."

Her mother smiled at me before stepping off to the side, and I held out my arm. I ushered Bella in first before I followed in stride, listening as her mother closed the front door behind us. My eyes drifted up the stairs to see if we had any more company before we ventured into the kitchen, and their charming home struck a chord with my heart that I knew would never unsound itself.

There wasn't anything about Bella's life that I didn't want to be part of. And that included being involved in her parent's life.

"How do you take your coffee?" her mother asked.

"Black," Bella and I said in unison.

I peered down at her with a smirk and watched her cheeks blush.

"He takes it black, Mom."

Her mother giggled. "Wonderful, that makes it easy on me."

I reached for my mug as she picked it up. "Need any help with the cake? I've heard I cut generous portions."

Her eyebrows rose. "Well, in that case, you can cut all three of us a nice slice."

Bella shuffled her way to the freezer. "Who wants ice cream?"

Her mother's hand shot into the air. "Me! I do! Do we have any whipped cream left in the fridge?"

Bella opened the door. "Yes, we do. Oooooh, there's straw-berry syrup, too."

I placed my hand on the small of her back. "I'd love to have some syrup on mine. Would you like some on yours?"

She looked up at me, fluttering those eyelashes of hers. "Yeah, I'd love some."

I patted her back. "Great. I'll get it. You go sit with your mother."

I sliced up the cake and divvied up ice cream before bringing all the condiments to the table. And as we dug in, I had a wonderful conversation with Bella's mother. For as unpleasant as her father had been, her mother made up the slack. She was easy to speak with, easy to make laugh, and easy to entertain. With every word she said, I saw the passion behind her eyes. Every time she mentioned Bella in any form, her soul ignited through her words. I could tell she loved her family, despite how chaotic it seemed to be.

But, there was still a lingering tension that wouldn't release itself.

"So, Wyatt. What do you do at your parent's company?" Mrs. Lancaster asked.

Bella leaned forward. "It's not technically their parents' company anymore."

Her mother nodded. "Oh, oh, oh. I'm sorry for the confusion."

I placed my hand on her forearm. "It's okay. Everyone makes that mistake at least once. The transfer of ownership regarding the company is still fairly new, and it wasn't as if we made a big deal about it."

Bella jumped back in. "But, to answer your question, he's the CIO."

Her mother furrowed her brow. "What does that stand for?"

I pushed my empty bowl away. "Chief Investment Officer."

Her mother took another big bite of ice cream. "And what does that mean? What is your role in the company?"

"Well, I oversee our board of investors, I make sure our stock doesn't become volatile on the open market, and I make sure all of the company's outgoing money toward business purchases nets us a decent-enough profit to justify the cost."

Her eyebrows rose. "Sounds like a big job."

I chuckled. "It's less convoluted than it sounds. It's a lot of number-crunching, organizing, and dealing with old, whiny man-babies who want their money quicker than we can sometimes get it to them."

Bella giggled. "I had a run-in with one on my first day with a Mr. Blanchard. And my interactions with him were enough to appreciate what Wyatt does daily."

Her mother snorted. "I can only imagine. I swear, grown men are sometimes more spoiled and pitch more fits than toddlers ever do."

"Is that right?"

Mr. Lancaster's groggy voice filled the kitchen, and everything came to a grinding halt. My anger kicked up in waves, but I swallowed it down as I stood. All eyes turned to him and his crooked body as he stood in the doorway with hair that looked almost damp.

Be the better man. Show him up with kindness.

"Wyatt," Bella whispered.

I patted her shoulder softly as I gathered the dishes from the table. I walked them silently over to the sink and placed them at the bottom before I turned to face her father again. His eyes followed me everywhere I went, so I made sure to make a show of cleaning up the table. Wiping down the stickiness that had gotten left behind. I made sure to show him precisely the role he should've played in their lives as a man who didn't work and didn't bring in a cent to help out his family. Because someone sure as hell needed to show this guy how to act. I even dared to walk over and kissed Mrs. Lancaster's cheek before quietly thanking her for the cake and ice cream. Then, I walked up to Bella's father and held out my hand for him to shake.

Hoping—and praying, to be honest—that he'd take the fucking olive branch so we could all move forward from this nonsense.

21

Bella

I watched Wyatt hold out his hand, and I held my breath. My mother's grip on my knee strengthened, and, oddly enough, it gave me a bit of hope. She wouldn't be freaking out so much about this of her own accord if she didn't like Wyatt. And getting Mom to like anyone outside of her small circle of friends was a monumental task, in and of itself.

But, my father didn't reach for his hand.

It felt like time had slowed to nothing. It felt like every second that passed tugged along with it an eternity of years that threatened to mock me. That threatened to remind me of the pitiful life I lead and that I'd always—always—be stuck with my parents. The idea sank my heart. The idea of living my life without Wyatt forced tears to brew behind the backs of my eyes.

Since when did I start caring so much for him?

My mind scrambled at a blurring pace. Part of me wanted to hop up and step in front of Wyatt to shield him from what I knew was coming. And yet, the other part of me wished with all my might that my father would finally be reasonable. I didn't care about his beef with Wyatt's father because that had nothing to do with Wyatt. Whatever went on between Dad and Remington, Sr. had nothing to do with us or our future.

"Please, Dad. Come on," I whispered.

Then, the unthinkable happened. I watched it in slow motion as if a movie crew had filmed it specifically for me. I watched my father's hand rise before he gripped Wyatt's. My jaw hit the floor as Mom patted my knee so furiously that I knew it would leave a bruise behind. My eyes panned over to Wyatt's face, and he was beaming from ear to ear as if he'd just won the war of the century. My eyes darted back to my father, and he still didn't look pleased. But, they were shaking hands, and that meant something, especially when my father was involved.

"Take a seat," Dad said.

Wyatt nodded. "Of course."

Dad dropped his hand, and the two sat down across from my mother and me, respectively. Wyatt's foot slid against my own, his leg reaching out for me to comfort me as my father sat across the table. My father kept his eyes locked on Wyatt, and he didn't seem to mind one bit. My stare volleyed between the two men, waiting for one of them to break the tension-filled silence.

Then, Dad spoke. "You been drinking?"

Wyatt nodded. "Two whiskey neats."

He chuckled. "Needed the courage to come over?"

Wyatt clasped his hands in his lap. "Can you blame me with our track record?"

Dad's face twitched. "I'm pretty protective of my daughter."

"As you should be."

"How's she doing at work?"

"She's doing above and beyond what we expected."

Dad crooked his eyebrow. "That because of her work? Or other things?"

Wyatt held his gaze. "Work, most definitely. Outside factors don't have a bearing on her job."

"Good."

"Yes. Very good."

Mom giggled, and I swatted at her, but I knew what she was thinking. Holy fucking hell, my father and Wyatt were way too much alike. I mean, the way they spoke to one another. The way they carried themselves in an unfamiliar conversation. The way they both gravitated to alcohol in order to give themselves courage. Even down to their posture, they were similar. My father, with his legs crossed at his ankles, and Wyatt, with his leg crossed over his knee. Both of them, with their hands folded in their laps. Both of them, with unwavering gazes.

The resemblance was uncanny.

And I had no idea what that said about me.

Dad puffed out his cheeks with a sigh. "You been seein' my daughter?"

Wyatt peeked over at me as if to get permission. So, I nodded my head. This conversation had to happen sooner or later. So, we might as well get it out of the way.

"Yes, sir," Wyatt said as he turned back to Dad, "I'm seeing your daughter."

Dad harrumphed. "You treatin' her right?"

Wyatt peeked over at me again, and it broke my heart. The idea that he didn't feel right in answering that question all by himself showed me the kind of talk we needed to have after this was all said and done. My father's gaze dancing between the two of us. I saw Wyatt's question behind his eyes.

So, I reached out and smoothed my hand down Wyatt's arm before taking his hand in mine. "Yes, Daddy. He's treating me wonderfully."

Dad scoffed. "Why'd he have to look at you like that, then?"

I looked at him. "You want the real answer?"

Wyatt's hand clenched mine tightly as Dad nodded. "I do."

I crooked an eyebrow. "Even if you aren't going to like it?"

He sighed. "Hit me with it."

I sighed. "You were right. Wyatt and I have been sleeping together. Only, he didn't know I was a virgin before it happened. He feels like he took something from me that wasn't rightfully his, and I've been trying to reassure him that I picked him for a reason."

The room went dead silent. I heard Mom gasp as her jaw unhinged, and the fire behind my father's eyes was unmistakable. But, I didn't release Wyatt's hand. I didn't abandon his side as my parents digested the information I had just thrown at them. I mean, I'd never necessarily been secretive with either of them. But, we also weren't the kind of family to talk about such things as openly as I just had.

Wyatt scooted his chair back a bit to get closer to me, and I leaned forward to kiss the shell of his ear.

"Relax, I promise it's okay," I whispered softly.

Dad drew in a very, very deep breath. "I suppose I asked for it."

I nodded. "You did."

Mom rubbed my shoulder. "You okay?"

I peeked over at her. "Oh, I'm great. I'm the happiest I've ever been in, well, ever."

Mom smiled. "That's what it's all about, honey. That's what it should be about, anyway."

Her statement made my eyes gravitate back to Dad. "Yeah, it should be."

Dad sucked air through his teeth. "So, you slept with my daughter?"

Wyatt shook his head. "No."

I furrowed my brow. "What?"

Dad lifted his chin. "What does that mean, son?"

Then, Wyatt laced his fingers with mine. "I made love to your daughter, sure. If we really want to get into it. But, I'm not just sleeping with her because she's not just some girl you hook up with and then call a cab for the next morning. She's greater than that. She's more than that."

My eyes watered as my gaze danced against the profile of his face. "Do you mean that?"

He turned to look at me. "I said it, didn't I?"

Dad chuckled. "At least he's a man of his word."

Wyatt smiled softly. "We can talk about this later if you'd like. We don't have to do it now."

I nodded slowly. "I think that might be warranted."

Dad cleared his throat. "Got one last question for you, though."

Wyatt turned back toward him. "Hit me with it."

Dad leaned forward. "What the hell are your intentions with my daughter?"

I thought the room would come to a grinding halt again. I thought that silence would fill the air while Wyatt searched for the appropriate words to keep this curt conversation balanced on the hairpin trigger without exploding the roof off of the house. But, there wasn't a skipped beat. There wasn't a moment of silence. Wyatt answered that question as if he had been prepared for it his entire life, and it pushed tears down my cheeks.

"Mr. Lancaster, I have every intention of dating your daughter. I have every intention of making sure she's as comfortable at work as possible. I have every intention of taking her out Friday after work for coffee that will hopefully spiral into an early dinner every week. I have every intention of making sure she falls in love with me so I'm not the only one in that spot."

"Oh, my goodness," Mom whispered.

Dad chewed on the inside of his cheek. "Love, huh?"

Wyatt nodded. "I'm in love with your daughter, sir. And my intentions are that of a man who never wants to let that go if I can help it."

I felt a tear streaking my neck. "You—you love me?"

He turned to face me before he cupped my cheek with his free hand. "I do, Bella. I love everything about you. And as time goes on, here's how I see this plan working out. You ready?"

I nodded, but I was stunned, speechless, and oblivious to the fact that we had an audience for our most intimate conversation to date.

"I plan on taking you out every Friday night. I plan on spending my lunch hours with you in my office just so we can have more time to talk. I plan on promoting you to my personal secretary just so I can move you upstairs and see you more often, and one day I plan on hearing you tell me how much you love me."

I drew in a broken breath. "Oh, Wyatt."

He leaned closer. "I plan on proposing, Bella. I plan on marrying you. Waking up every morning to you. Starting a family with you. I plan on giving you everything you've ever wanted, and then some. And I plan on doing it with both of your parents' approval. I plan on all of this and more because you're deserving of all of it. My only hope is that you can accept my plan. Can you, Bella?"

I heard Mom squealing into her palms as she covered her mouth. I saw my father out of the corner of my eye hanging on to every word Wyatt spoke. And I felt his presence with me, next to me, guiding me through a phase in my life I never thought I'd reach.

Tears poured down my cheeks as I tried to find the strength to speak. But, Dad beat me to the punch.

"If you hurt her in any way, son, I'm coming for you. And no security officers you put at that place where you work is gonna stop me. You got that?"

Wyatt nodded, even though he kept his eyes on me. "I got it."

Dad grunted. "I'll do it sober, too. Make sure I don't miss the shot to your head."

I sniffled as a soft giggle fell from my lips. "Daddy, geez."

"Look at me, princess."

I forced my gaze to his. "Yeah?"

I watched his face soften as he drew in a breath through his nose. "You're my little girl. You're my *only* little girl. And

I'm not just gonna give you over to anyone. You know that, right?"

"I swear he's a good man, Dad."

He nodded slowly. "I can see that."

"So?" Wyatt asked.

I panned my gaze back over to his stare. "Yes?"

He leaned in even closer. "You think you can handle that plan?"

I smiled softly. "Under one condition."

"Name it."

I pointed at Dad. "We don't get married until he's sober for the wedding. I don't want him walking me down the aisle smelling like vodka."

Wyatt smirked. "Deal."

I held his hand tightly as he faced my father once more. "Mr. Lancaster?"

Dad nodded. "Yep?"

"I'd like to ask your daughter out on a formal date. Is that all right?"

Dad peeked over at me before he smiled. "Yeah. That's all right."

I squealed with delight as Wyatt stood to his feet. He brought me with him, clutching my hand as he brought it to his lips to kiss. I felt my cheeks flush as Mom clapped her hands. I saw my father beaming from ear to ear out of the corner of my eye.

Then, Wyatt tucked a strand of loose hair behind my ear. "Bella?"

"Yes, Wyatt?"

He licked his lips. "Will you go out with me tomorrow night?"

I giggled with delight. "I'd love nothing more."

He captured my lips with his own, and Mom started belly-laughing in a way I hadn't heard in years. Even Dad chuckled as my arms slipped around his neck. I never wanted to stop kissing those soft, pillowy lips of his. I never wanted to be apart from Wyatt ever again.

I loved this man.

And I wanted to spend the rest of my life at his side.

Mom stood to her feet. "Would you like to stay for a movie or something, Wyatt?"

Dad groaned as he stood as well. "I'm sure he's got a lot of work to get done before tomorrow night. Right, son?"

Wyatt pointed at him. "Actually, he's right on that one. Got about twenty folders of stuff to work through before I come to pick you up."

I started searching for my purse. "Here. Let me find something to write my number on for you."

Wyatt grinned. "No need."

I furrowed my brow. "Why not?"

He shrugged. "How do you think I found your house? Everything's already in your employee file."

Dad threw his head back in laughter, and Mom quickly joined him. I shook my head in disbelief as Wyatt stood there, his arm wrapped around my waist, and a grin plastered across his cheeks. I let my hands run down his chest. I felt the beating of his heart against my palms before I stepped farther into his embrace. And as I leaned my head against his chest, I felt his arms blanket me away from the world before he kissed me on top of the head.

"I'll see you tomorrow around six. That sound good?" Wyatt whispered.

And with a nod of my head, we solidified our first *official* date plan.

🦋 22 🦋

Wyatt

I straightened my tie and slid my hands down the buttoned-up suit coat I had chosen for the evening. The all-black ensemble was single-handedly my number one to-go power suit in my closet. But, it felt a little intimidating for a date. So, I plucked a pale yellow pocket square off my closet wall and slid it into the pocket, taking in the softening effect the color had against the all-black palette. I grinned as I slid my onyx cufflinks into place. I opted for a solid-black watch Ryan had given me as a birthday gift a few years back, completing the smoldering outfit I had chosen for Bella this evening.

Then, after winking at myself in the mirror, I headed for my truck.

The drive passed by slowly, and I grew impatient as I wound my way toward Bella's parents' place. I prayed to any god listening that they hadn't given her a hard time over anything today because if her father spoiled this for her, I'd be the first to wring his neck. I had to respect him, sure, but that didn't mean I had to tolerate his drunken antics.

Especially when those antics hurt the woman I love.

My heart blossomed at the word. Love. It was a word I never thought I'd attribute to anyone on this planet who wasn't one of my brothers. I had kept away from that kind of life because I knew how distracting it could get. I mean, I was seeing that distraction pour forth in the lives of my brothers in real-time. Keeping up a relationship was just as much work as my chosen career path, and sometimes that hard work didn't always pay off.

I didn't like placing bets when I wasn't sure if I'd win.

But, with Bella, things were different.

"Here we go," I murmured.

I saw curtains ruffling upstairs as lights started flicking on in Bella's house. I pulled into the driveway, and the door swung open, revealing her father as he stood perfectly upright. I grinned to myself as I parked my truck. I kept the engine running as I walked onto the porch. And as I stuck my hand out for her father to shake once more, I expected the stale smell of beer to waft in my general direction. But that night, I didn't smell it.

"Wyatt. Glad to see someone can be on time."

I chuckled. "You look good, Mr. Lancaster."

He dropped my hand. "Yeah, well. Ran out of beer."

I slid my hands into my pockets. "The look suits you. You should consider making it a weekly thing."

He chuckled before the pitter-patter of feet came rushing down the steps. When Bella's mother appeared in the doorway, she practically lunged at me. She wrapped her arms around my neck, giving me the biggest hug I'd ever received from someone I wasn't having sex with.

Then, Bella appeared in the doorway, and my arms went limp.

"My God," I murmured.

Her hair had been curled and swept up into a gorgeous French twist that donned little sparkling pearl-like gems that seemed to grow right out of her hair. Her dark-green dress shimmered in the moonlight, falling softly off her shoulders and framing her curves in a way that made my cock jump. The cinch in her waist guided my eye down her legs, where I saw pumps on her feet that not only exposed her impeccably-groomed toes but flexed her calves. Her ass look rounder as she gave me a soft twirl.

"Too overdressed? I kept telling Mom that I was much too overdressed."

Her mother swatted my arm. "Tell her she looks phenomenal."

I reached out and gripped Bella's arm softly, stopping her in her tracks. "You look breathtaking, Bella. Really."

When she smiled up at me, my soul took flight. It felt as if I were soaring through the clouds without a worry in sight. I offered her my arm without another word spoken, and she wrapped hers around my own, allowing me to usher to my truck before I offered her my hand and helped her into it.

"You have her back at a decent time now!" her father exclaimed.

I waved at him. "No later than midnight, I promise!"

"Make it eleven!"

I chuckled. "Eleven thirty, but that's my final offer!"

The man gave me a thumbs up before his wife finally pulled him inside, and that left me my chance to whisk Bella away from all of her worries. We drove to the restaurant in silence, her eyes falling out the window toward the passing landscape while her fingers interlocked with mine. But, once we got into the restaurant and sat down at our private table, I snapped my fingers.

Then watched as our waiter for the evening placed a perfectly wrapped red-and-gold box with a black bow in front of her.

"What's this?" she asked.

I smiled. "Open it and see."

I watched her painstakingly open the present, taking great care not to rip the paper or tear the bow to shreds. She was meticulous in everything she did, and I admired that about her. She never let haste or impatience get in the way. She always thought with a rational mind, even if she didn't feel as if she were in control of the situation at hand. I liked that about her. I always believed that a woman should know how to keep herself poised in the right circumstances and know when it was okay to let loose.

And when she finally got the box open, her eyes watered. "Wyatt."

I crossed my leg over my knee. "Do you like it?"

She plucked the pearl necklace from the velvet encasement. "What in the world did you do?"

I folded my hands in my lap. "I bought you a gift. I saw it in a shop window a couple of days ago and thought it would look beautiful on you while you're working."

She snickered. "I can't accept this. This is too much. This thing probably costs more than my paycheck!"

I nodded. "You'd be right about that."

Her jaw gawked farther as I continued, "But, that doesn't mean you don't deserve it. I wanted to get you something nice. So, I hope you'll find reasons to wear it."

And as I sat there, ogling her beautiful curves and valleys in the dim firelight, I watched her slide the string of pearls over her head.

Before she double-wrapped it and let the excess linger against her cleavage. "Like this?"

I swallowed hard. "Just like that. It's perfect."

Our waiter approached the table. "Pardon the intrusion, but I have a wonderful appetizer here. Iced oysters with a butter sauce, marinara on the side, and two glasses of wine that pair wonderfully with our oyster selection. Shall I begin pouring?"

I didn't register the question as Bella's face paled. The

only thing I focused on was the quick way she pushed her chair away from the table. I waved the waiter away, trying to get him to take the tray of seafood out of the room. But, it was no use.

As quickly as the oysters had come out, Bella moved with speed unbeknownst to her before she puked in her purse.

"Oh, my goodness," the waiter said breathlessly. "Here, let me get you some water. And some more napkins."

Panic rushed my body as I calmly stood to my feet. "Give my condolences to the chef, will you? I'm afraid we're going to have to cancel the evening."

The waiter stumbled over his words. "Y–you do know that —I mean, just because—the check, it can't—"

I rushed to Bella's side. "Charge whatever you need to the card on file. We have to leave."

I scooped a heaving Bella into my arms as her stomach continued to jump. I rushed her out of the private room into a sea of cacophonous smells that caused her to gag once more. I shoved myself into the first restroom I could find and walked her over to the sink, where she tilted her head off to the side and threw up once again.

"Hey! This is the girl's room!" a woman exclaimed.

I growled beneath my breath. "And once my girlfriend is done puking in the sink, I'll be out of your hair."

The woman behind me harrumphed, and I wanted nothing more than to lay into her with my words. But, my sole concern was getting Bella out of there. The wide look in her eye told me that this had caught her off-guard. The way her skin kept paling told me she needed a doctor.

"Can I move you?" I whispered.

And when she nodded, I shoved us back out into the restaurant.

After getting her laid down in my lap in the front seat of the truck, I rushed us to the hospital. Her dry-heaving was disconcerting, especially since she seemed to not have anything else to bring back up. My mind ran with a million different worst-case scenarios, none of which abated my growing fears.

Nevertheless, I kept my opinions to myself as I charged us through the ER doors.

"I need help!" I exclaimed.

Two nurses rushed up to me with a wheelchair, and I shook my head.

"She needs a gurney. She can't sit up. She can't stop heaving. She only stops when she's laying down, kind of."

Bella groaned. "Help."

A man's voice called to the left of me. "Got a bed here!"

I turned toward him and met him halfway down the hallway. "Thank you so much."

The nurse who brought the wheelchair ran up to my side. "When did it start?"

I ran my hand through my hair. "At dinner, maybe thirty minutes ago? The oysters came out and she just started throwing up."

The man in the white coat started taking vitals. "So, she ate oysters and got sick?"

Bella groaned. "I wanna go home. Where's Mom?"

I shook my head as I caressed her sweating brow. "No, she didn't ingest them. She just looked at them and boom."

"Wyatt, please."

I looked down into her tired eyes. "I'll call your parents. Where's your phone?"

She pointed to her purse, and I wrinkled my nose. "Right. Okay, what's your home number? Do your parents have a landline?"

She sniffled. "What's wrong with me?"

I kissed her damp forehead. "I don't know, but we aren't leaving here until we have an answer. Now, what is your parents' number?"

After she rattled it off to me, the doctor and nurses whisked her away. I jogged alongside her, maneuvering myself down hallways and around corners until they shoved us into an impossibly small room. The nurse quickly set an IV and got her started on fluids while the doctor took her temperature and started feeling around her jawline.

And down her neck.

And around her abdomen.

"Does any of this hurt?" the doctor asked.

Bella shook her head softly. "No. Not even my stomach hurts. That's why I don't—"

The telltale jolt of her chest caused me to scramble, and I got a cup just in front of her before she sat up and vomited once more. I rubbed her back and smoothed her hair away from her face, hoping to minimize how much of it she got on herself. After Bella flopped back down to the bed, I saw one of the nurses hand me a pen and a pad of paper. And, as if we were on the same wavelength, I wrote Bella's parent's number down so the nurse could call them.

Then, I turned my attention back to the doctor. "Do you have any ideas as to what's going on?"

The doctor shook his head. "I don't like the theorize without tests. But, we can do four easy ones right now with nothing more than a simple blood draw. That's where we're going to start."

Bella sighed. "Just take me home. It's been a really stressful time, and this is probably just my body getting rid of the bad juju."

I slid my knuckles softly against her pale cheek. "Just entertain my worries a bit. I'm footing the bill for the ER visit anyway, so it won't cost you anything."

She blinked. "Are you sure?"

I nodded. "I'd rather be really safe than really sorry, all right?"

A nurse rushed back into the room and slid a thin needle into one of the open ports on the IV tubing. "Here, this will help calm down your gag reflex so you will stop dry-heaving endlessly. It might make you drowsy, though. So, do what you can to stay awake. Depending on how these tests come out, we'll need you conscious for imaging."

I licked my lips. "I can do that, thank you."

Bella's gag reflex choked her up again. "How long until it starts working?"

The nurse pushed on the plunger slowly. "For some people, it's less than five minutes. For others, it's close to fifteen. It all depends on the body's chemistry, but rest assured it will work."

That seemed to settle Bella down, and for a few minutes, I got her to relax. But, as every minute ticked by with no change in her dry-heaving, I saw her grow panicked again. I brushed my fingers through her hair and tried to calm her. I placed kisses all along her forehead and jawline in an attempt to get her flustered enough to push some color back into her cheeks.

Nothing I did helped, though.

And after thirty minutes, the medicine still hadn't kicked in.

"Wyatt?" Bella asked.

I held her hand tightly. "Yes? Everything okay?"

She heaved a bit before talking once more. "Shouldn't you be calling someone? Since you're here with me?"

Oh, shit. Boone. "Actually, yes. I should. Hold on."

I pulled my phone out of my pocket and stood to my feet. I quickly dialed Boone's number and hoped to God on high he hadn't made it to the restaurant yet. I eased myself out of the room and leaned against the painted concrete block wall, watching as doctors and nurses rushed around like chickens with their heads chopped off.

Then, Boone finally answered. "Hey, everything all right?"

Ryan yelled in the background. "We're loadin' up now!"

I blinked. "What the fuck is Ryan doing there?"

Boone chuckled. "You know he's going stir crazy while their house is being built. Apparently, that guesthouse Bryce has isn't set up for a family of four."

Ryan called out to me again. "You bet your fucking ass it isn't!"

I sucked air through my teeth. "Boone, I need you to listen. This evening is called off."

He paused. "Wait. Why? What happened?"

"I can't get into it right now, but Bella and I are in the ER. The two of you need to get to the hospital, pronto."

I heard rustling around on the other end of the line before Ryan's voice sounded. "What hospital?"

I pinched the bridge of my nose. "The only one in the damn town, man. Conroe Regional. And I need you guys here ASAP."

"Why? It sounds like you have an idea of what's going on. Care to rope us in?"

Anger shoved the words out a little too loudly. "Because when you fuck your secretary, sometimes she gets pregnant. So for fuck's sake, get your asses down here and help me keep calm!"

"What the hell did you just say, boy?"

The growling voice was accompanied by a hand wrapped around my throat, and as Bella's mother gasped, I felt her father put me into the wall. He squeezed his hand around my throat as my cell phone fell from my hand, clattering to the ground as Ryan's voice sounded through the speaker.

"Wyatt! We're coming. We're like, ten minutes away!"

And as I gazed into the fiery, angry eyes of Mr. Lancaster, I didn't know which was worse—the fact that he had heard what I said or the fact that I was pretty sure I was right.

23

Bella

Everything around me fell silent. At one point, I was having blood drawn and my cheeks swabbed. And in the blink of an eye, I was in a darkened room with cold gobs of goo on my stomach. I felt someone squeezing my hand, and I looked up only to see Wyatt's startled face. His jaw was unhinged in shock as something moved around my clammy skin. I lobbed my head over and saw the technician's lips moving, but no sound came out of her mouth.

Then, I looked at the screen.

The black and white screen with a little bulbous dot dancing around in a massive circle.

Out of nowhere, a loud and rapid thumping hit my ears. It

pulled me out of my trance, and all the sounds around me bombarded my ears at once. I heard the technician say something about "how far along" I was. I felt Wyatt clinging to my hand as soft pants fell from his parted lips. I closed my eyes and relaxed against the unforgiving exam table with a million questions swirling through my mind.

But, the question that panicked me the most came flying out first. "What the hell am I going to tell my parents?"

A tear slid down my cheek, and something warm and strong brushed it away. I tilted my head to the side and gazed up at Wyatt's hand as it moved back to his side. He dipped down, tucking a strand of hair behind my ear as he gazed into my eyes.

Then, he spoke the words that made me sick to my stomach again. "They already know, Bella. They got here about forty minutes ago when the nurses were still rushing around to do the tests."

I bolted upright. "I have to get out of here."

The ultrasound technician rolled backward in her chair as her wand clattered to the floor.

"Bella, you need to lie down. It's going to be okay. I've already talked to—"

I swung my feet over the edge of the table without bothering to pull the bottom of my shirt out of my bra to cover my stomach again. "Dad's going to kill me. This will compromise my job, and that job is the only thing keeping my family afloat. I can't be pregnant. I have to get out of here. I can't be a single mother. Not yet. I don't have the means to—"

Wyatt gripped my shoulders. "Bella!"

His staunch voice halted me in my tracks, and tears streaked my cheeks. "Why is this happening?"

He crooked his finger beneath my chin and pulled my gaze up to his. And when our stares connected, I saw something sort of like determination behind his eyes. Determination and hurt. Like I had slapped him in the face, but that slap provided him with even more fuel.

Then, the words I had spoken finally registered. "Wyatt, I didn't mean to assu—"

Before I could even get the apology out, his lips fell against mine. The kiss was soft but heated. And when his arm snaked around the small of my back, he scooped me against his suit. I felt the squishing of that gel against the expensive fabrics he wore. His tongue slid along the roof of my mouth, calming my racing heart. With every touch of his tongue against mine, I felt more centered. More grounded. More clear-headed than before.

Then, he pulled back and stared me down. "First of all, you won't ever be a single mother. So, cut that shit talk out right now."

I blinked. "So, you're staying? After all of this?"

He grinned as he slid his hand along my hair. "I wouldn't have it any other way at this point, Bella. I love you. And I meant those words when I said them."

I sighed with relief. "I don't know how it's possible in such a short amount of time to feel this way, but I love you, too, Wyatt."

He captured my lips again and allowed his hand to explore. He cupped the back of my head before massaging the nape of my neck. His hand slid down my spine before finding the crook of my waist. And just as the thought crossed my mind that I couldn't possibly love this man anymore, he outdid himself.

He pressed his hand against my bare, goopy stomach and smiled against my lips. "I love you both so much," he whispered.

"I don't give a shit what you say. I'm seeing my daughter now!"

I groaned. "Oh, no."

Just as I heard my father kicking up a stink outside, the door to the exam room burst open. With wild eyes and hands flailing everywhere, I heard my mother booking it down the hallway to try to catch up to him.

"You leave those kids alone!" Mom exclaimed.

The sonographer stood to her feet. "I'm sorry, sir, but only those who are sanctioned to be in here are allowed in the ultrasound rooms."

Dad's face turned beet red. "I'm sanctioned to be anywhere my damn daughter is."

Wyatt moved to cover my half-naked body. "Mr. Lancaster, we'll be done in a moment. Then, we can all sit down in Bella's room and—"

Dad pointed at Wyatt's face. "You listen here, and you listen good. Until you marry my daughter, I'm the one who speaks for her. I'm the one who advocates for her. And I'm the one who should be in this room. Not the man who knocked her up without a second thought because he leads with his dick and not with his head."

Wyatt's shoulders squared off. "I won't allow any more of your verbal abuse to grace my ears or the ears of the woman I love. Now, turn around and walk out before I pick you up and put you out there in that hallway."

I drew in a deep breath. "Everyone, just shut up!"

I panted for breath as my stomach started heaving again. My chest and my throat lurched as Wyatt backtracked quickly and began tracing circles on my shoulders. He blew softly on the nape of my neck to get my heated body to cool down, and the entire time my eyes stayed locked with my father's angry glare.

Until they panned over to the ultrasound screen.

The second his eyes beheld the still-life pictures of the small sack on the screen, his frown faded. The redness of his cheeks receded. Hell, even his posture relaxed. I watched as my father walked over to the screen, and when the ultrasound technician stopped him, I held up my hand.

"It's okay. That's his grandchild. Let him see," I said.

Mom was crying softly in the corner, blotting her skin with a tissue. I watched silently as my father moved to the screen and pressed his fingertips against it. His eyes danced along the black-and-white image, and he looked as if he had just witnessed God with his own eyes.

Then, he turned to me. And tears crested his tired stare.

"There he is!" someone exclaimed.

The door burst back open, and two men with "security" written on their chests started wrangling my father. I reached out for him, and he tried to take my hand, but they quickly tucked his arms behind his back. Dad growled and bucked against them as I cried out for them to stop. To let him stay. To let him stand beside me so he could hold my hand for this moment.

And out of nowhere, Wyatt bellowed, "Stop it, right now!"

The entire room came to a standstill before Wyatt looked down at me. "Ready when you are."

I smiled up at him. "Thanks."

He cupped my cheek. "Anything for you."

I looked back over at the security guards. "My parents can stay. They have every right to be here, and they should be here. But, Dad?"

"Yes, sweetheart?"

I turned my head to look up into his face. "One outburst and you're done. This is happening, whether you like it or not, and things are going to be very different from here on out. You want to be in this child's life?"

His hand took mine. "You have my word that things will change."

Then, my eyes fell back on the ultrasound technician. "Can we let them listen to the heartbeat?"

She patted the table, indicating I need to get back up, and then she picked up the wand from the floor and sanitized it. "Of course. We aren't done with the ultrasound anyway. Ready to lean back? I'll have to put more gel on your stomach."

I nodded. "Ready when you are."

With the help of Wyatt and my father, I leaned back against the exam table. I squealed a bit when the cold gooiness hit my skin, but with both of the men I loved at my side, I knew nothing could go wrong. Mom slid my feet out of my heels and began mindlessly massaging them, looking for something to do with her nervous energy instead of chewing on her nailbeds like she always did.

And when she pressed that wand against my stomach once more, that rapidly beating sound filled the room again.

Bringing tears to all of our eyes.

"My God," Dad whispered.

"Hello there, little one," Mom said breathlessly.

My lower lip quivered. "I promise things will be better for you."

Wyatt leaned down, kissing my forehead before he murmured against my skin. "Things will be better for all of us."

Dad sniffled. "You're gonna be a fantastic mother, Bella."

My chest jumped with a sob. "You really think so?"

He chuckled as he stared down at me. "I know so. Trust me, I know so."

Wyatt squeezed my hand. "So do I."

And when I looked up at him, I found him staring at my father instead of me.

"Got something to say, son, spit it out," Dad said.

Wyatt straightened his back. "I want you to know that I'll never leave them, Mr. Lancaster. No matter what happens and no matter where life takes me, if it doesn't benefit them, it won't happen. And even if Bella and I don't work out—"

"Hey," I said softly, "don't put that out there."

He squeezed my hand and continued, "I come from a divorced home, sir. And while my father did the best he could, there was always that absence. I don't talk a lot about Mom leaving, and I don't plan on doing it now, but I want you to know that even if things sever Bella and me, our child won't ever wonder what it's like to have a father. I won't be that absent parent. You have my word."

Dad's jaw quivered before he nodded. "Good. Does my heart good to hear that."

I drew in a broken breath. "What about the rest of the Remington family, Dad?"

He peered down at me. "What about them?"

I released his hand and started rubbing his arm. "You can't carry around the kind of anger you've been holding on to. Not when I've become, physically, part of their family."

His lips turned into a frown before he nodded. "I hear you, sweetheart, I hear you."

Then, my father's eyes rose to Wyatt's. "Consider this the start of turning over a new leaf with your family and mine. Let's don't fuck it up."

I rolled my eyes and shook my head, but Wyatt simply took it in stride.

"I won't, Mr. Lancaster. None of us will."

The ultrasound technician spoke up. "I take it you guys want pictures?"

My father's eyes didn't waver from Wyatt's face. "As many as you can give us."

Wyatt kept staring at him, too. "Can we get a sound file with the baby's heartbeat on it? I got a gift to give a man who's going to make an awesome grandfather."

And as the technician prepared everything for us, I felt a heavy weight lift off my shoulders.

Leaving me more room to jerk and jolt before I leaned my head over the edge of the chair and vomited onto the floor.

❊ 24 ❊

Wyatt

I brushed Bella's hair back from her forehead as we waited for a wheelchair. "How are you feeling, beautiful?"

She smiled up at me. "Ready to go home and get some sleep."

"Well, about that..."

The nurse pushed a wheelchair into the room. "Here ya go! It's the protocol for you to ride out of the ER in one, but once you're outside, you can get up and walk as usual."

I held out my hand and steadied Bella as she eased herself into the chair. Her hand trembled, and I knew she had to be hungry. It was damn near ten o'clock at night, and if I was feeling faint from a lack of sustenance, then I knew she had to be feeling rough, especially since she was growing my child.

"So, what about my sleeping at home?" Bella asked.

I started rolling her down the hallway. "I thought you could spend the evening with me. You know, so I can keep an eye on you."

She giggled. "Don't bring oysters around me, and I should be just—" She dry-heaved in the middle of that sentence, and, to me, it was all the proof I needed.

Her parents had a long way to go in terms of shaping up before they'd be able to take care of Bella the way she needed, and I could provide her with all of that and so much more.

Dammit, I'm gonna need a bigger place.

"All right," she said breathlessly as I pushed her through the automatic metal doors, "maybe just for tonight."

I kissed the top of her head. "You're going to move in eventually, so you might as well stay the weekend so we can go house shopping."

Bryce's voice was the first to hit my ears. "No worries! We've already got you a plot of land carved out at the Rocking R Ranch."

I snickered. "Sorry, guys. As much as I'd love to be part of this weird family compound, I'm going to have to pass for now. We need to be in a place we can make our own before this baby comes along, and not a second beforehand."

Ryan came over and clapped my back. "Ever the different one, huh?"

Bella giggled. "And he's perfect the way he is."

Boone walked up and puffed his cheeks out with a sigh. "Dude, I know you're a private man and all, but this is a bit much, don't you think?"

All of us started laughing as I held my hand out for Bella. I helped her out of the wheelchair before I passed it off to be wheeled back inside, and the second I turned my back, a throng of squeals reverberated throughout the space we occupied. Bella's parents had done a good job of ushering us off to the side so that we weren't blocking the entrance to the ER, but the second the girls parted the crowd, they made their way straight for Bella.

Every. Single. One of them.

"Oh, my God! This is going to be fantastic. We have to have a girl's weekend," Willow said.

Luna nodded vigorously. "Oh, and snacks. Once you get through the nausea, we need to have a bunch of snacks to munch on for our girl's weekend."

Ellie laughed as she shoved her way forward. "Also, massages. Pregnancy massages are an absolute necessity, especially for us short girls. There's more pressure on our hips than ever before, and it's going to suck in a few weeks."

Sadie started digging around in her purse. "Here, you should carry some of these. They're ginger hard candies, and they worked wonders for me on the days where I was more nauseous than others."

Ellie nodded. "I think I still have some leftover ginger suckers as well. So, if they work for you, don't hesitate to come by, and I can pass them off to you."

I whistled low and turned to face Bart. "Mrs. Weatherford's earning her paycheck tonight, isn't she?"

He chuckled. "Let's just say it's essentially double overtime, considering the nature of the emergency."

I squeezed his shoulder. "I really appreciate you guys being here."

Bryce barked with laughter. "After the phone call you made to Boone that practically made him shit himself, it shouldn't shock you that we all showed up."

"My boy. Where's my boy?"

The second I heard Dad's voice rise above the crowd, I froze. My eyes immediately darted over toward Bella's parents as the chaotic sounds ceased to exist. Dad and Mom shoved through the group of people before they wrapped their arms around me. Mom was on the verge of tears, and Dad kept squeezing me as if this were the proudest moment of my life that he'd ever born witness to.

But, I was too concerned about Bella's parents to take it all in.

"Mom. Dad. I didn't know you guys were going to be here."

Dad held me out by my shoulders. "When all of our children are rushing to the hospital, you bet your ass, we know about it."

Mom patted my cheek. "Don't think you're too old for me to spank that ass of yours, either. You should've called us after you called Boone."

I sighed. "I didn't want to worry you guys, especially since my focus was on Bella. She's got this dry-heaving thing that just won't quit."

"Wyatt?" Bella asked softly.

I immediately turned my attention to her. "What is it? Are you okay?"

She pointed to the bulge in her cheek. "This ginger candy tastes phenomenal. And it's settling my stomach."

I grinned. "That's wonderful. We'll pick some up tomorrow. Ellie?"

She typed away on her phone. "Already putting a reminder in my calendar. I'll send Ryan over with the suckers first thing in the morning."

I nodded. "I really appreciate it, thank you. Just bring them over to my place. Bella and I will be staying there for the weekend so we can go house-hunting."

"How are you doing with all of this, Mr. Lancaster?" Dad's voice pierced through the crowd again, and I held my breath.

He approached Bella's parents, and I braced myself for a stand-off. I readied to come to my parent's defense while Bella had one foot pointed toward her parents. And for a brief moment, I wondered if we'd all be at odds for the rest of our lives. I wondered if Bella and I would ever stand on the same side when push came to shove.

However, instead of starting into a fight, Bella's father held his arms wide open, and the two men embraced.

"What the *fuck*?" I whispered.

Bella gasped. "Oh, my God."

I bent down toward her ear. "This is good, right?"

She nodded slowly, her voice at a whisper. "Very, very good."

It shocked me to my very core to see these two men embracing. But, more than that, it astounded me that Bella's father was the one to initiate it. I wasn't sure how to feel, or what to think, or even what to say. So, I simply wrapped my arm around Bella's waist and tucked her close to my side.

Just in case the two men decided to show their asses anyway.

"How you doin', Lancaster?" Dad asked.

Bella's father nodded. "Been better but hope to get back there soon. You?"

Dad nodded slowly. "Eh, trying to adjust to retirement."

He chuckled. "Not going too well?"

Dad shrugged. "Too much free time. I need something to do with my life."

"You not racing anymore?"

Everyone could've heard a fucking pin drop a mile away the second that question was asked. But, Dad took it in stride when he shook his head.

"Nah, haven't raced since the rodeo cost me a friend. Ain't nothin' in this world more important than friendship. And I figured if it happened once, it would eventually happen again."

Bella's father nodded very slowly. "You didn't trip me up, did you?"

Dad's eyes widened. "What? No! Is that what you've thought all this time? I didn't even know you were injured,

Lanny. Because if I had known? I'da been the first one at your side. I'da stopped that damn rodeo myself and dragged you out of the way."

"Lanny?" Bella asked.

Mom giggled. "Once upon a time, these two were pretty close."

Bella's mother snickered. "Those two were always battling for the top slots in just about every race they shared together. So, naturally, we always got together to poke fun at one another and psyche everyone up for rodeos that were around the corner."

My jaw dropped open. "So, you guys were friends."

Dad shook his head. "No. We were best friends. And I hope we can be that again, one of these days."

Bella's father drew in a deep breath, trying to keep his tears at bay. "I think maybe we can get there. You know, with some time."

Dad held out his hand. "Shake on it?"

Bella's father chuckled as he took the man's hand. "I'll shake on it, sure."

I hugged Bella against my body and listened as she sniffled. She wiped tears away from her eyes, and I hoped, for our child's sake, that this was the beginning of something spectacular. Having families at war with one another never did anyone any good. And the only people who paid for shit like that were the helpless children who didn't have a choice as to what family they were born into. I prayed, for our child's sake, that new leaves started turning over tonight.

"I love you," I said. I peeked down at Bella and watched her smile as she gazed up into my eyes.

"I love you too, Wyatt."

I smiled before I dipped down, capturing her lips for the softest kiss imaginable. My heart exploded with delight and dripped with joy as she turned into me. Her hands slid up my chest, settling against my heartbeat as it quickly ticked up. I blanketed her back and held her close. I let my tongue explore a bit of her lips before I pulled away. And as I tucked a loose strand of hair behind her ear, I lost myself in the beauty of her brown eyes before my brothers started patting me on the back.

"There you go."

"Good damn job, dude."

"She's a good one. Don't fuck it up."

"Congratulations. Now, the real work begins."

"Don't scare him off now. Ease him into things."

I kept my eyes on Bella as I smiled. "Nothing could scare me away from this. Not when my family is involved."

The woman I loved let out the biggest yawn, and I scooped her into my arms. She squealed before she curled up, tucking herself close as I suspended her in midair with nothing but my arms. I looked over at Bella's father, and he nodded toward me, giving me silent permission to whisk his daughter away.

And after looking everyone in their eyes to silently thank them for showing up tonight, I started toward my truck.

"I don't want to leave you," she murmured.

I chuckled. "Trust me; you're never leaving me. I hope you know that."

She let out another yawn. "Should we have asked Dad for permission before just taking off?"

I snickered. "We're pregnant, Bella. The time for permission has long since passed. Not that it really worked in the beginning in the first place."

She let out a tired giggle. "I suppose you're right."

"And just so we're clear, you don't answer to me, either. You are your own person. Your own woman. And as long as you don't make massive decisions without me, you don't need to ask me to do things. Just keep me updated and fill me in. That's all I ask."

She snuggled closer against my chest. "You're so perfect."

I unlocked my truck. "Hardly. But, I'm perfect for you, and you're perfect for me, and that's all we need."

"Mmmmmhm."

She yawned yet again as I set her down quickly to open the door. I helped her up and quickly jogged around to the side as our families dispersed back to their own vehicles. I was excited to have Bella with me for the weekend but even more excited for us to go house-hunting. I'd been searching for an excuse to snatch up one of these older homes to renovate, and I couldn't wait to find the house that was perfect for Bella and me to raise our family.

"Where do you live, anyway?" Bella murmured.

She leaned her cheek against my shoulder, and it dawned on me how little we knew about each other. I started chuckling at the idea, but that chuckle grew into laughter. And by the time we hit the main road that parted Conroe in half, I was damn near wiping tears away from my eyes.

"What's so funny?" she groaned.

I wrapped my arm around her tired body. "Absolutely nothing."

"Then, why are you laughing?"

"Because we're pregnant, and you haven't even seen my place yet."

She snickered. "Yeah, that is kind of funny."

I kissed the side of her head. "It's not much right now, but that's because I've been saving for a big house restoration. A lot of these homes around here are historic and beautiful, and they're just waiting for the right person to come in and renovate them to their former glory."

She yawned deeply. "As long as I don't have to do anything, I'm good."

"I mean, you might have to go furniture shopping."

Her head lifted from my shoulder. "I can do that."

I barked with laughter. "I figured you'd like that. Come here, gorgeous."

We weaved our way through town until I eased myself into the townhouse complex where I resided. It wasn't much to look at, and it certainly didn't have all of the amenities I wanted out of a home. But, it was a cozy little place that served as a nice "in-between" home until I found the permanent one I wanted to settle down in.

And when I eased into my assigned parking spot, Bella drew in a deep breath.

"I never saw you as a townhouse kinda guy."

I quirked an eyebrow. "Oh, really?"

She shook her head. "No. I saw you as a loft man. Or, a studio apartment that's kind of minimalist in style and is all gray-scale."

I cut the engine to the truck. "Then, you're gonna freak out when you see the inside of this place."

She slowly turned to face me. "Why?"

I unbuckled my seatbelt. "Come inside and find out."

I wasn't sure why I was nervous about ushering Bella into my home, but I had to clench my muscles in order to keep my hands from trembling. I pressed my palm into the small of her back as I led her into my townhouse, and her eyes bulged as she slowly walked down the short hallway that dumped straight into my living room.

"Holy shit!" she exclaimed.

I locked the door behind me. "Do you like it?"

She pointed at the bay window in my living room. "Is that stained glass?"

I hung up my keys. "Not technically. It's a sheer overlay I purchased in a store one day. I thought it would add a nice conversation piece without breaking the bank. So, I put it up myself."

She shook her head slowly. "You're a stained-glass kind of guy."

I walked up beside her. "What can I say? I'm full of surprises. Oh, by the way, we're totally having a stained glass window put in our living room of whatever home we purchase."

She pointed to the couch. "Is that leather?"

I nodded. "Genuine leather. Painstaking to take care of but worth the effort."

"You can coat those with some sort of waterproofing thing, right?"

"Yes, you can. Why?"

She ran her hand along the back of the couch. "Because this would be great for kids. It looks very nice, it feels comfortable, but with that waterproofing stuff on it, it wouldn't soak up spills and stains like microfiber couches."

I grinned. "Already thinking about baby-proofing, huh?"

She looked up at me. "No reason why we can't have nice stuff that's also baby-friendly."

I cupped her cheeks. "You're amazing; you know that?"

Her cheeks blushed. "I might be amazing, but I'm also tired."

I kissed her lips softly. "Then, let's get you upstairs. I can't wait for you to see the California king-size bed."

She groaned. "Oh, that sounds like heaven."

I pressed my lips to her ear. "It's got memory foam."

She sighed. "My hero."

I lowered my voice to a whisper. "Cooling memory foam."

She groaned. "Pretty sure I just came."

I threw my head back and laughed. "Come on, silly girl.

Let's get you into a comfy shirt of mine before we climb into bed."

And when my fingers laced together with hers, I felt the whole of my world drop into place. Bella felt like home. It felt like I had finally found home.

My Bella. Our child. And our family's legacy.

That was what I had been missing all this time.

EPILOGUE

Bella
Six Months Later

"Ugh, come on. Just get on the damned—there!"

I released the picture and watched it sway for a few moments, but when it stopped, it hung perfectly against the wall. I waddled backward and rested my hands on my protruding stomach, feeling our bouncing baby boy kicking around inside me.

The picture was the finishing touch on the nursery.

Things were well with Wyatt and me. My morning sickness finally alleviated itself five months into the pregnancy, and ever since then, I'd been craving the weirdest things. This morning, it was hazelnut spread and bananas on buttered toast, and for lunch, it was macaroni and cheese poured over barbecue potato chips.

And as I stood there, staring at the beautiful 3-D ultra-sound picture of our sweet boy, I suddenly got a craving for a juicy red pepper and a thick chocolate milkshake.

"Wyatt!" I exclaimed.

I heard him rushing up the steps before he skidded into the nursery. "You okay? What's wrong? What can I help with?"

I giggled as I pointed at the wall. "Look. That frame you picked up is perfect."

He walked over toward me and faced the picture. "Hey, that turned out really good. Especially centered over his crib like that."

"It's why I pulled the crib out from the wall a bit. I know you don't like that three-inch gap. But, if that picture ever comes down, it'll slide to the floor instead of falling into the crib."

He kissed my temple. "You always think of everything. I don't even know why I question you sometimes."

I shrugged. "I don't know why, either."

He chuckled before he turned me to face him. "So, what's the real reason why you called me up here?"

I snorted. "That obvious, huh?"

He pointed to his cheek. "You got a little drool there. Just —just a drop."

I wiped at my mouth. "I do not. Seriously?"

"Just a bit. Just—you just missed it."

I kept wiping at my face. "Is it gone? Wyatt, get it for me! Please?"

He kissed my forehead. "I'm just playing with you. You aren't drooling on yourself."

I pushed him playfully. "Jerk."

"Beautiful." He winked.

I blushed. "I was hoping we had a red pepper downstairs?"

He paused, racking his brain. "I think we do, yeah. I used one for our salad last night, but I believe there's still one left."

"And we still have chocolate ice cream?"

He wrinkled his nose. "Don't tell me you're going to dip the red pepper in the ice cream."

My stomach growled. "Actually, I was just gonna make a shake, but your idea sounds much yummier. Let's go."

I took Wyatt's hand and dragged him out of the blue and yellow nursery before we eased our way down the stairs. The beautiful historic country-style home we had built nestled just on the outskirts on the upper corner of Rocking R Ranch. And yes, Wyatt had once been against it. After all, he was the kind of man that needed his space. But, when we thought about how left out our child might feel when all of his cousins lived in the same area and we were clear across town, it didn't take much to change his mind on the matter.

So, we paid expediting fees to get the house up and running as quickly as possible.

Granted, there was still a lot to be done. The house still had bare bones in some places. But, all of the rooms we functioned in routinely had been put together first. Our master bedroom was a behemoth of a space, and both of us each had our own walk-in closets. Our en-suite master bathroom not only had a jetted tub, but it had a stand-up shower with a waterfall shower head that felt like I was taking showers in the middle of a rainforest. Our kitchen was done up with beautiful marble floors that matched the countertops strewn across the house, all of the appliances were that fingerprint-resistant stainless steel, and our son's nursery had a bathroom attached to it as well so he could grow up and have his own space with his own privacy.

And yes, Wyatt had a massive stained-glass bay window built directly in the living room.

At first, I thought the damned thing was going to be gaudy. But, it actually turned out pretty tasteful. It sat deeply enough for there to be a nice, cushioned, reclined seating area, but only the side windows were stained-glass. The enormous middle window looked out over the backyard that would eventually be landscaped to hold numerous fruit trees, beautiful patches of flowers, and a cobblestone walkway out to a gazebo that would sit right next to the creek flowing into the forest that separated us from the rest of his family.

And every time I sat in that window, I was in awe of the life we had.

"Wyatt, look! Another deer!" I pointed out the kitchen window as he sliced up a red pepper on a plate for me.

"If I hunted, I'd have a field day with this property," he said through his chuckling.

I whipped my head in his direction. "Well, maybe since there's always deer wandering up into our backyard, we can finally get your parents over here regularly."

"They've got, like, a gazillion grandchildren. They make their rounds and try to divvy up their time as much as they can. After all, it's why they moved back from Italy in the first place."

I sighed. "I know, I know. I just like having them around. They're lots of fun."

Wyatt slid the plate of red pepper slices in my direction. "Things still rocky with your dad?"

I shrugged. "They're not really rocky, per se. But, you know, getting sober is tough. Some days, he's fine. Other days, he's so angry that Mom's calling me crying and begging me to come over."

He kissed my cheek. "I'm glad you have the strength to tell her 'no,' beautiful."

I plucked a slice from the plate. "It's not that I don't want to. I just don't want to fuck with my blood pressure right now. Everything I feel, the baby feels, and I want our child to have as healthy of an environment as possible."

He rubbed my back. "And that's one of the many reasons why I love you."

I smiled. "You know why I love you?"

"Why?"

I bit into the red pepper slice. "I love it when you do what you're going to say, like getting me some chocolate ice cream so I can dip these suckers."

He wrinkled his nose. "Even though you're gross, I still love you."

"And even though you pee sitting down in the mornings, I still love you, too."

He backtracked and pointed at me. "Hey, it's either that or peeing all over the walls. And I wasn't sure if you wanted to clean that shit up or not."

I barked with laughter. "Who says I'm cleaning it up, Mr. PeePeeWalls?"

His laughter filled the kitchen as I leaned against the counter. I watched him pull out the chocolate ice cream and whip up a little bit in our blender before he poured it into a dipping container for me. I salivated at the taste as I dunked my red pepper slices into it. I moaned with every bite and practically wolfed down the snack.

And like the wonderful man he was, he grabbed another pepper and started slicing.

"So, are we still on for hosting Sunday family dinner in a couple of days?" he asked.

I nodded. "Yep. And my parents RSVP'd to this one, so let's cross our fingers that Dad can keep it together."

"No drinking until they're gone then. Got it."

"That'll be the only downside to us hosting."

He shrugged. "Bah, my family won't mind. If you noticed, we actually didn't have alcohol at Bart's last week. Or Bryce's, the week before that."

I blinked. "No, we didn't, did we?"

He shook his head. "Trust me. The entire family is rooting

for your father. And we wouldn't want to jeopardize his progress."

My eyes watered with tears of happiness. "You're amazing. You're all amazing; you know that?"

He smiled at me as he slid me another sliced-up pepper. "Amazing begets amazing. Remember that."

I wolfed down the other red pepper before deciding to call it quits. I grabbed a bottle of water from the fridge before I walked outside and eased myself into a comfy chair. I cracked open the bottle and took a few swigs, watching the deer at the corner of the property drink from the creek.

And pretty soon, Wyatt sat beside me as hammering sounded from inside the house.

"They just arrive?" I asked.

I saw Wyatt nod out of the corner of my eye. "Yeah, I let them in just as you walked outside. They're finishing up the last guest bedroom before heading into the basement. They're going to get the waterproofing started before they throw up a ceiling and all that stuff."

My head tilted off to the side. "Have you heard back from Bryce and Will yet?"

"About what?"

I scoffed. "What do you mean, about what? You know, just a little thing called 'buying out your investors.' That thing you've been burning your tires out on these past few months. Have they given you an answer yet?"

He shrugged. "These kinds of things take time. They haven't said 'no,' so that's promising."

"Has there been a hiccup on their end or something?"

"Personally? I think Bryce is down, but Willow is hesitant. She's more conservative when it comes to money and things, and I think Bryce is having a hard time convincing her about how much it'll cost to buy out their portion of the company."

"What do you think about Will?"

He paused for a long time before he sighed. "Will doesn't think that buying out our board is such a great idea. Especially since we don't have proven profits from the refinery yet. He thinks they should stick around as our 'get out of jail free' card if this shit tanks and goes south."

"I mean, he's got a good point there."

I heard something rustling in the bushes, and I peered over my shoulder, but I didn't see anything. Wyatt kept talking at me, but I could've sworn I heard what sounded like footsteps.

Then again, the construction workers were in the house. So, maybe it was one of them walking around outside.

"Bella, you okay?" Wyatt asked.

I turned my head to face him. "Sorry, I just thought—I... heard..."

My jaw dropped open when I found Wyatt down on not one but both of his knees. He stared up at me with a smile on his face that warmed my soul before he held up the most beautiful ring I'd ever seen in my life. The entire world around me stopped. Every single sound faded into the background, save for the sound of my heart beating in my ears.

And when Wyatt's lips started to move, I concentrated on his words.

"Bella, you've changed my life completely. You're giving me something I could have never given myself, and in the process, you've somehow decided that I'm the one you want to be with. I don't know how the hell I got so damn lucky with you stumbling into my world the way you did, but I promise never to break your heart, never to betray you, and never let you go so long as I live."

"Wyatt," I whispered.

He held my left hand in his. "Bella Lancaster, will you do me the absolute honor of becoming my wife?"

I nodded. "Yes. Holy shit, Wyatt, yes!"

He slid the ring onto my finger, and I leaped up, tackling him to the ground. He wrapped his arms around me and quickly rolled me over so I wouldn't fall onto my stomach, then his lips crashed heavily against my own. Tears slid down the side of my face. And as the sounds of the world around us came rushing back to my ears, I didn't hear the banging of hammers and the pitter-patter of working feet.

Instead, I heard the sounds of hands clapping and people whistling. Others cheered, and still more yelped for joy.

And when Wyatt finally got up and helped me to my feet, I saw my parents rushing for me.

"Mom! Dad!"

They both wrapped me up tightly and kissed my cheeks.

"We're so happy for you," Mom whispered.

Dad left a lingering kiss against my forehead. "You've never looked happier, and I couldn't be prouder."

"Who wants pizza?" Bart called out.

I turned around and saw our entire family flooding our backyard. Bryce and Willow with their kids. Ryan and Ellie with their brood in tow. Luna and Bart fought with one another over what pizzas to order, and Boone stood there with a grin on his face and his hands slid into his pockets.

Even Sadie and Will were there with their little ones, despite the fact that Sadie hadn't been feeling well these past few days.

"Where did you guys come from?" I exclaimed.

Wyatt wrapped his arms around me from behind. "I texted them yesterday and told them what was happening."

I pointed to the side of the house. "Who was walking around over there? Who did I hear?"

Bryce raised his hand. "The little one got away from me. Almost spoiled the whole thing, too!"

We all erupted into monumental laughter as I leaned against Wyatt. The father of my child. The love of my life. And now, my fiancé.

"I love you so fucking much," I whispered.

He gripped my chin and turned my eyes up to his. "And I love you, Bella. Always."

And it sure as hell didn't get much better than this.

Follow Boone and Kate's journey to their HEA in Cowboy's Accidental Wife.

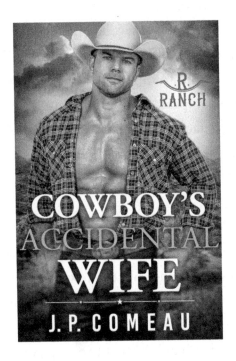

Made in the USA
Middletown, DE
09 October 2021

49968524R00126